Invisible Walls

Chandrika Balan

Invisible Walls

Translated from Malayalam by the Author

THORNBIRD
NIYOGI BOOKS

Invisible Walls: English translation of Malayalam title *Aparnayude Thadavarakal* by Chandrika Balan, originally published by DC Books, Kottayam, 2013.

Published by
NIYOGI BOOKS
Block D, Building No. 77,
Okhla Industrial Area, Phase-I,
New Delhi-110 020, INDIA
Tel: 91-11-26816301, 26818960
Email: niyogibooks@gmail.com
Website: www.niyogibooksindia.com

Editor: K.E. Priyamvada
Design: Nabanita Das
Cover image: Original painting 'Transparent', oil on canvas,
by Rajasekharan Parameswaran

ISBN: 978-93-86906-32-8
Publication: 2018

Printed at: Niyogi Offset Pvt. Ltd., New Delhi, India

“

You are about to begin reading Italo Calvino's
If on a Winter's Night a Traveler.
Relax. Concentrate. Dispel every other thought.
Let the world around you fade.

—The opening lines of Italo Calvino's
If on a Winter's Night a Traveler

“

I had listened joyously to several Ramayanas sung by great poets;
In none of them had Srirama left for the forest without Seetha.

—Seetha's words to Srirama, Ayodhya Kanda,
Adhyathma Ramayana

Contents

The Beginning

Kamala-1

Kamala was the first passenger to enter the compartment. She found her cabin, sat on her reserved lower birth and stretched her legs celebrating her freedom, wondering who would be the other three passengers sharing the cabin with her. While travelling, she always hoped that nobody came to the cabin with little kids. Satanic kids are more than enough to spoil a person's journey. All the crying, noise pollution, fights with one another, beatings from the parents' side, followed by moral counselling ... ugh! The disgust born of observing all this had made Kamala and her three university friends take a decision not to have children at all. Kamala and her friends, firebrand researchers in the Delhi campus, call themselves FOURCENTRIC. Two men and two girls living together without believing in family or parenthood have raised many eyebrows. But they don't care.

A young man entered Kamala's cabin and placed his suitcase on the upper berth. So he belongs to the upper class, Kamala smiled to herself, thinking of the campus railway lingo.

He sat on the window seat opposite Kamala's, opened his tote bag and took out a book. Kamala read the title—*The Selfish Gene.* She noticed that his jeans and her leggings were of the same colour. He adjusted the earphones of his iPod and casually looked at her. When he found that she was also looking at him, he liberated his ears and smiled.

'Hello! I am Govind Bhaskar. You must be Kamala, right?'

The reservations chart was pasted outside every compartment; so any passenger can get to know the co-passengers' names and pretend to be a magician.

'Yes. I am Kamala.'

'Are you a student?'

'Yes.'

She took her mobile and called her friend, a clear indication that she was not interested in continuing the conversation.

'Hi Sidan, I have boarded the train ... No, the train hasn't started yet ... Missed you a lot, da ... Tell you all that after I reach. Have patience, man ...'

The fellow traveller listened for some time and, feeling bored, put his earphones back in and opened *The Selfish Gene.*

And then a husband and wife entered the cabin, filling the entire space. Kamala felt happy that they did not bring their children. The couple sat face to face, the wife on Kamala's side and the husband on the man's side. They seemed to be careful not to look at each other.

Kamala opened her handbag and took out the book she had brought to read.

Invisible Walls

by

Chandrika Balan

Before she could start reading, Sidan's call came for her:

'You ass, why did you ring off without replying? Is there any problem? Is your dad alright?'

Kamala lowered her voice, 'My father is perfectly ok, Sidan. I couldn't speak to you from home. So many people were there. Everything was a well-organized trick—to make me come home.'

Sidan laughed. 'Oh, yet another drama? Did anyone come to see the bride?'

'Over my dead body,' said Kamala and laughed.

'OK, OK. Come soon. All of us are waiting to hear the story.'

Kamala sat for a while looking out through the window. How can one accept an extremely traditional society that refuses to understand the individual? As James Joyce has said, one is in chains right from the time of birth, be it that of religion, family or the nation. The Fourcentric gang has broken most of the chains to be together, but chains still follow them.

The train started moving forward and Kamala opened the book.

Invisible Walls

Part I

The Train

Chapter 1

The Passengers

Aparna is a passenger in a train now. Absorbed in Yukio Mishima's *Confessions of a Mask,* she pays no heed to the noise around. For a brief moment she takes her mind off from the book, though not the eyes, to think of the author. She had reached the lines *'What I wanted was to die among strangers, untroubled, beneath a cloudless sky ... What I wanted was some natural, spontaneous suicide.'* Her mind wandered from the text to its author, Yukio Mishima, who turned his own death into a performance, drawing a dagger with both hands across his stomach and spilling out his intestines. The ritualistic *hara-kiri.*

Imagine there was such a ritual in our own country; it would be girls who would do it naturally and spontaneously. Aparna visualised a row of girls standing poised with daggers in hands. They are 'survivors', to use the journalistic lingo. During her brief vacation in Kerala, Aparna had noticed the rising rate of girls here victimised by the lustful other sex. In Delhi too, the graph is always on a sharp increase. From the abdomens of the girls who commit *hara-kiri* tender embryos may jerk out on to the feet of the onlookers. Maybe one of them would land at the feet of its progenitor.

Aparna bit her mind instead of her lips and went back to the novel. A vendor opened the door of the air-conditioned cabin and asked if she wanted jasmine flowers. Withdrawing the eyes raised to him, Aparna threw a glance at the young man sitting opposite her, concentrating on his laptop. He was in a mechanical world into which no fragrance of jasmine flowers would penetrate.

'No, thanks,' Aparna said to the jasmine-man.

He smiled in a meaningful way and addressed the young man, 'Sir, why don't you buy jasmine flowers for madam?'

The Laptop-man did not even bother to look up. Had he looked up, this story might have become a romantic one at this point itself.

Pushing the jasmine-man from behind, a mother and two kids entered the cabin. The jasmine-man glared at them, but moved away without trying to sell jasmine flowers, maybe because the woman had worn tight-fitting jeans. The girl in red shorts and white tee shirt shouted aloud their seat numbers and charged at the Laptop-man. When she squeezed herself between the window and the Laptop-man, saying, 'This is our seat,' he had to move away from the window, rather helplessly. The mother sat near Aparna with the other girl, while the coolie pushed a huge suitcase under the seat.

'Hey, be careful,' the lady said. 'It has costly crockery inside. Don't break them.'

Aparna turned back to the novel. She never liked women who travelled with crockery and kids. This lady is a modern one, clad in jeans and tee shirt; yet her bag contains only crockery and she has noisy children with her, in the typical way.

'Chinnu, sit straight.' She raised her voice. 'Put your legs down.'

Aparna understood that red shorts plus white tee shirt is Chinnu. Chinnu put her legs down, looked at Aparna and feigned a smile. When she did not get a smile in return, Chinnu removed the smile from her face and looked away.

On most of her train journeys Aparna had found the child co-travellers to be a nuisance. She could never be the woman who fondles strangers' kids with 'What is your name?' or 'Which class are you studying' or 'Auntie will give you sweets if you sing "Baa baa black sheep."' On the rare occasions she had tried to do it, she had failed miserably.

'Minnu, don't do dirty things,' the Jeans-mom told her second daughter.

So blue shorts plus white tee shirt is Minnu! Aparna looked at her to see what dirty deed she was doing. The heinous crime was sucking of the thumb. Jeans-mom tried to pull her daughter's thumb from her mouth. Minnu, in her efforts not to let it go, bit on the thumb and started howling with pain.

'There goes the pleasure of my trip,' Aparna said to herself.

Pahle he kya ... sang Jeans-mom's mobile exactly at that minute. She took out the mobile from the pouch on her belt and started talking, while her other hand dexterously pressed Minnu's mouth and turned the howling down to half-volume. She told the person at the other end that they had boarded the train, that the train would start soon, and that there was no problem. Her voice was so loud that she did not seem to require the services of a mobile phone at all.

As Aparna returned to the *Confessions of a Mask*, and as Jeans-Mom kept on talking, and as the Laptop-man went on hitting the keyboard, Minnu stopped howling, liberated herself and moved towards Chinnu. Within minutes, with a loud scream Minnu landed on the lap of Aparna, and Aparna's novel landed on the floor.

Only then did the Laptop-man raise his head.

'Hey Chinnu!' shouted Jeans-mom. Then she informed the person at the other end of her mobile 'Hell, they are fighting. I will call you later.'

With a 'Sorry,' Jeans-mom took Minnu from Aparna's lap and turned to Chinnu. 'What do you think you are doing? Why did you quarrel with her? Why did you throw her like that? I want an answer just now!'

'She wanted my window seat. I won't give it.'

'Why? Why won't you give it? Did you bring the window seat when you came? Will you take it with you when you leave the train? No? Then how can you say it is yours?'

Aparna saw with surprise that though the woman was clad in jeans, it was great Indian philosophical truths that were coming out of her.

After the public trial, Jeans-mom gave the verdict: 'Give the window seat to Minnu. Say three times to her "I am sorry."'

Maybe because she knew there would be other reasons to be sorry if she does not obey, Chinnu did what her mother wanted and peace was restored to the cabin. The Laptop-man returned to his machine.

The train had started moving while all this was taking place, and it slowly gained speed.

Jeans-mom opened her shoulder bag and distributed food packets to Chinnu and Minnu. And then she started darting looks at Aparna with sly smiles. Aparna understood the symptoms immediately and pretended to be immersed in the book. The kids were eating cylindrical sausages covered in silver foil with relish.

'Won't you have your dinner?' Jeans-mom asked Aparna. The veteran traveller that she is, Aparna knows that women who open a conversation like this at night will have their eyes on the lower berth. So she curtly said 'I had dinner from home' and concentrated on the novel.

Suddenly the Laptop-man jerked up and took out his mobile. Aparna wondered why she had not heard the ringtone; maybe it was on vibratory alert. He listened for a while to the voice at the other end and then said, 'No, not like that. I will tell you. Please correct those lines.'

Then he sang in a deep voice in a low key:

Garlands of jasmine fell on the hill of hymens.
The dark and lonely hill, the Virgin Hill.
From there roared one thousand virgins
On nights, scaring the passers-by.

Aparna raised her head with curiosity.

'Mahesh, do compose it carefully, ok?' He said into the phone 'It is the first time that my poem appears in that prestigious journal. Please... ok? ...What? Where has the train reached? I don't know. Does it matter?'

He put the mobile away and went back to his laptop.

Aparna felt her curiosity rising. So this man is a poet! But now who is not a poet? Everyone writes poems. But she liked the usage 'hill of hymens.' Instead of 'garlands of jasmine' he should have used the word 'wreaths.' She also liked his last question: *Does it matter?*

Quite right! Once you have got into the train, all you have to notice is whether it has reached the station where you have to get off. So many stops and stations in between! Who cares!

Does it matter?

Does anything matter?

Chapter 2

Goodbye Till we Meet Again

When the train stopped at some station, the Jeans-mom took Minnu by force to the toilet. Taking her chance, Chinnu moved closer to the Laptop-man and looked closely at the screen. Your pseudo-concentration is going to have a break, Aparna smiled secretly.

'Uncle,' Chinnu called him sweetly. But her call came back to her like a ball bouncing against a wall.

'Uncle, do you have Donald Duck cartoons here?'

'No,' said the Laptop-man curtly.

'Garfield?'

'No.'

'Superman? Spiderman? At least Doraemon?'

'No.'

'Then why do you carry this stupid thing around?' Chinnu became angry. 'This cricket game you are watching is really stupid.'

So this man was only watching cricket! As Aparna looked on, he shut his laptop, removed his earphones, put them all up on the upper berth and walked out of the cabin without looking at anyone.

Chinnu visibly turned into a monster as she twisted her lips and gritted her teeth. She called after him: 'Not only cricket, but you who watch it are also stupid—like my Papa.'

Then with a sudden frenzy she started going up the stairs to the upper berth. Smelling danger, Aparna got up, asking her, 'What are you doing, girl?'

'I am going to throw his computer down and break it into two.'

'No,' said Aparna and instantaneously caught her to prevent her from going up further. Chinnu who had already mounted two or three steps, pulled herself away from Aparna with unusual vigour, all the while kicking at her. The kicks delivered by the red-socks-covered little feet were really painful. Aparna held her forcefully and looked at the door of the cabin, wishing fervently that the Jeans-mom or the Laptop-man would come soon.

'What is it to you if I break that computer?' Chinnu shouted at Aparna. 'You bitch, it is not yours.'

The door was opened by the Laptop-man who stood with his bottle of mineral water, startled at the scene. 'Come, please,' Aparna yelled at him. 'Save your laptop from this girl.'

The Jeans-mom came only after that. Chinnu had to tell the Laptop-man three times 'I will not touch your computer again; I am sorry,' and tell Aparna three times 'I am sorry I used bad language.' Then she dumped herself on the seat and sat with a tightened face. Till the journey ended the next day, she never even looked at Aparna, nor did she talk to her.

But the Laptop-man spoke to her at 9.48 pm.

'I understand that your name is Aparna.'

'How did you understand?'

'I knew it already from the seat allotment chart outside.'

Aparna just smiled.

Both of them were lying on the upper berths when this conversation took place. Though Aparna had vowed not to let her lower berth go, she had to yield to Jeans-mom at her words, 'Ok, if you won't give it, I will sleep with Minnu on the upper berth. But let me tell you something. Usually Minnu urinates so much in her sleep that her diaper leaks. Don't jump at my throat if that happens.'

Aparna had no desire to be woken rudely in her sleep by foul-smelling drops of urine falling on her face. So she scrambled up in haste to the upper berth.

Covering her body with the railway shawl, Aparna lay trying to read Yukio Mishima. The Laptop-man was just lying flat on the other upper berth with the laptop on his chest, watching a movie. Must be a movie as serious as the spectator. Not even a momentary reflex of laughter could be seen on his face.

It was when he tried to raise his head that he saw Aparna trying to peep into the laptop. He smiled at her and she returned it warmly. Then he removed his earphones and the conversation ensued. He asked her name, etc.

'Which movie is it?' Aparna asked.

'Turner and Hooch.'

Aparna had seen the movie. The comedy created by the mismatch of the freak detective Turner and the dog Hooch had made her laugh out loudly at several places. She wondered how her fellow passenger could watch it without any emotion.

On a sudden impulse she said 'Goodnight' to him and turned over to the other side. The Laptop-man was terribly disappointed. He had felt a soft corner towards the lady who had saved his laptop from the demon child. If she does not want his friendship, that is ok with him. But why did she say goodnight and turn away when he told her the name of the movie? Maybe she is the admirer of intellectual movies, the uninteresting sort that would go jostling at film festivals, chanting the names of Kim Ki Duk, Fellini, Bergman and the like.

He returned to *Turner and Hooch*. It was a church wedding scene. Hooch, recognizing a man in the crowd, was running after him and the man was trying to dodge him.

When Aparna woke up, the cabin was bathed in morning light. The young man on the opposite berth was snoring softly. The Jeans-mom vied with him from the lower berth with loud snores. Aparna lay idle for some time and then got down. Jeans-mom and Minnu were sleeping with heads in opposite directions; Aparna noticed that Minnu's diaper, which was quite visible, was dry! Jeans-mom and her children got up only when the train stopped at some station and vendors of food knocked at the cabin door. At the first opportunity that she got, Aparna retrieved her window seat. Taking out the packed sandwiches she had brought from home, she returned to Yukio Mishima.

The Laptop-man took more time to wake up. It was Chinnu's loud voice of protest against having to eat bread for breakfast that made him open his eyes and look down.

'I hate bread,' Chinnu was growling. 'Buy me *bhatura*.'

Jeans-mom pointed out that Aparna, much senior to Chinnu, was eating bread for breakfast.

'I don't care, I don't care, I don't care,' Chinnu shouted. Maybe saying everything three times runs in the family.

Jeans-mom shouted back that shouting was bad manners. The Laptop-man slid down into the world of bad manners and went out.

He came back with a newspaper and food packet and sat opposite Aparna. Aparna was careful not to look at him. The soft emotions roused by the cold night, blue light and the smile must end with the night. But he did not seem to have any such thought. In fact, after eating, he was in no hurry to take out his laptop.

As Jeans-mom was talking loudly on the phone and Chinnu and Minnu were quarrelling with each other, he talked to Aparna. 'What a noisy family! Nuisance to us, no?'

Aparna gave him a polite smile and continued reading.

'Do you want the newspaper?'

'No, thanks.'

The Laptop-man tried again to continue the conversation, but, disappointed, took out his laptop. When he opened it, Aparna relaxed.

As the train was about to reach their destination, he helped her to take out her bags.

'How long would you be here in Delhi?' he asked.

'I live here,' she told him.

'Oh, I am on an official visit. I will be here for three days.'

Aparna did not show any interest in his official trip or stay and so he asked again, 'What do you do here? Are you a student?'

'Does it matter?' Aparna asked mischievously. He looked at her as if he had heard those words recently and then lapsed into silence. Aparna recalled an SMS she had once received from an old friend. *All problems are stuck between the Mind and Matter. If you don't Mind, it doesn't Matter.*

He spoke again only after they got out of the train. A bearded man on the platform lifted up Chinnu who was laughing hilariously while Minnu stood with hands outstretched to him and whimpering. The Jeans-mom, resting her hand on the trolley that carried costly crockery, was looking on with a proud smile. See my family, what a happy one!

And then the Laptop-man asked Aparna: 'Where do you stay? I can drop you there. The car will come to pick me up from the company.'

'No, thanks.' said Aparna. 'I know very well where I want to go and how to get there.'

He went pale at the insult and left in a hurry, muttering: 'OK, then. Bye.'

We will see him again only in the second section of PART III. And then he will throw Aparna's words back at her.

Interval-I

Kamala-2

Kamala raised her eyes from the book and looked outside. Nature's face was reddening. Kamala had often felt that both man and woman would become sexy and bewitching at the approach of twilight. She felt her mind throbbing with an unknown anguish and took out her mobile.

Govind, in the opposite seat, was swinging in sleep. Head thrown forward ... then raised slightly, moving sideways ... Sometimes his head tilted backward and his mouth opened. But never once did he become wakeful or open his eyes. Even when the whole body turned to one side with the train's movement, the body automatically corrected its position; he did not wake up. Kamala watched him with surprise—how could anyone fall so deeply asleep in the sitting posture?

The Selfish Gene lay abandoned by his side.

She wondered whether she would meet him anywhere in the future, like the forewarning in the novel she was reading. She decided not to give him any sentence in this train journey to be thrown back at her later.

'Where are you Sidan?' Kamala asked. 'What a racket I hear!'

'I am in the department store to buy atta. We thought we would make chapatti for dinner, but when we looked, found that there was no atta.'

'Aha! I like it. Where is God Vinayaka?'

'Vinu is taking the wheat powder packets from the rack. I am looking for something ready-to-eat. Where have you reached?'

'Dunno. Does it matter?' She said, echoing the novel.

'Does anything matter?' asked Sidan, though he hasn't even seen the novel.

She laughed loudly and then Vinayak's voice came to her.

'What is there to laugh so much, girl? Are you going to get married? Now, now, don't jump at my throat. Sidan whispered it to me.'

'You idiot, why should I get married? What will marriage give me more than what the Fourcentric gang is giving me?'

'Love you Kamu. Umma,' Vinu too laughed. 'Now tell me the truth. Whom did you miss more—Sidan or I?'

'Ok, I will tell you. But before that you tell me this. Whom did you miss more—Devangi or I?"

'Defeated. Withdrawing unconditionally.'

'Ha, ha, ha. Love you. Umma.'

In the hangover of the talk Kamala looked around to meet the angry and scowling eyes of the man sitting opposite her. Suddenly he withdrew his eyes and looked away in scorn.

Kamala wanted to laugh louder. But when she saw that the wife was sitting with closed eyes, her lips whispering prayers, Kamala switched off her laughter. She looked again at the sleeping Govind and went back to Aparna's story: **Part II: The Campus.**

Part II
The Campus

Chapter 1

The Journey Within

'Come, just a wee little bit more,' said the Guide and led them on. A foul smell pervaded the whole place. The five people followed him, wondering to themselves if this was really Life.

'Oh, I can't stand this; I think I will faint,' said Pradip Lahiri to Aparna.

'You were brought up on princely comforts; that is why. In the place where I come from, dirty people and foul-smelling paths are everyday sights.'

'Did you see *that*?' Everyone looked at where Kashyap pointed his finger. A dark child was sitting on the side of the path and excreting with effort. A small ball fell down and live worms began scattering themselves.

Neela Kalyani turned and vomited on the side of the path.

'Kashyap, you should not have,' Pradip Lahiri was irritated.

Neela Kalyani broke into a sweat from head to toe and faltered. People squatting here and there looked ravenously at her brimming breasts.

'Bitch!' Bejoy Luxmi whispered to Aparna. 'She knew we were coming to such a place; yet why so much ventilation on the dress? Do you see them staring rudely? Hope they won't attack us.'

Neela Kalyani was always the hot girl of the campus. What Luxmi said was correct. Neela was wearing tight leggings and a very short top with a low cut neck. She could have dressed more soberly. The Guide had cautioned them, 'The place is really dangerous—especially to go with ladies. Though I am coming with you to show the way, you have to take care of yourselves.'

Aparna felt a fear stirring within her. The fear had entered her heart when a weird-looking man started walking after them, beating on a drum hung from his neck. When she turned back to look, he grinned, revealing tobacco-stained teeth, every inch of him looking diabolic. She shuddered and restrained herself from looking again. Fortunately he stopped to watch a woman who was bathing, half-clad, on the roadside. His drum beats synchronized with the rhythm of her dipper going into the bucket full of water and rising up in the air to shower her head.

'Hey, you said it is only a short distance; but how long had we walked!' Kashyap shouted at the Guide.

'It is there, *Saab*, just where the lane turns.'

'Want water?' Pradip Lahiri asked Neela Kalyani. Afraid of the germs that might fly in when the bottle is opened, she refused the offer.

And then they reached the turning in the lane.

There they saw a small hut hoisted on four stumps like the legs of chairs. There was a cot with coir matting placed in the front yard. On the blanket spread on it a man was sitting idly. The man they had come in search of. But he was different from the wildest of their dreams: a middle-aged man in a dirty loincloth and unclean torso, stubble on his face, forcefully emitting the smell of alcohol.

Aparna was struck by the intensity and wildness of the look in his eyes. Eyes, she felt, that could hypnotize anyone with a mere look.

The Guide signalled them to stop at a distance and went to the man. They stood watching the Guide speak with too obvious respect. Then he came back with a disappointed face.

'A problem, *Saab*,' he said. 'He had agreed to me then, but now he says he does not want to see anyone.'

'Why?' Kashyap raised his voice. 'We had agreed to all his terms. Gave in advance the money for alcohol and grass. Then what is his problem?'

'I cannot ask him, Sir,' said the Guide. 'I am scared.'

'Hell, what scared? What crap! If you had such a phobia, why did you consent to be the mediator? We could have got some other person very easily.'

The Guide was now doubly scared. Pradip Lahiri asked him in a gentle voice, 'Tell us, why you are so scared of him?'

'*Saab*, think of the sights you had seen on the way here. All men are his slaves, women more so. He keeps them content with alcohol, grass. He is the Master here. If he just snaps his fingers, you won't be able to leave this place with the ladies.'

'I want to sit down,' said Neela Kalyani in a feeble voice that sounded more affected than real. She looked as weak as the leaves of spinach, and was trying to control the vomit that was coming up with hiccups.

'Can we get a chair please?' Kashyap asked the Guide with genuine concern.

'Why stop with chair? Why not ask for a canopied bed?' Bejoy Luxmi was irritated. 'Make her sit on the ground, *yaar*!'

The Guide brought a flat piece of wood from somewhere. Kashyap unloaded Neela Kalyani on it, hoping that she would not notice the dirt on it. She was too tired to notice anything and sat on the wood and kept on spitting to a side.

'This is real cheating!' Pradip Lahiri pointed his finger at the Guide. 'You will not get out of this nicely. How much money had you taken from us! We will get back every penny with interest.'

'What can I do, *Saab*? How can I know that he would behave like a cheap chameleon?'

The people of the colony, curious by now, had started coming near them and standing here and there, listening. Aparna felt that it would not be safe to linger there long.

Just at that moment Kashyap called her. 'Hey Aparna, come. Let us try to coax him.'

Holding her by the hand, Kashyap walked towards the middle-aged man sitting, meditating, on the cot. Feeling them coming near, he raised his bloodshot eyes and a tremor ran through Aparna's spine.

'No time to talk today,' he said in Hindi with a strange dialect. 'Go, don't waste my time.'

'You don't have to talk,' Kashyap said with false humility. 'In fact we don't want you to talk at all. But we would like to share with you some of our doubts. Can we?'

'Say and be gone!'

'Well, we have travelled round a lot. This place is one of the most beautiful places we have seen so far. Dark green woods! Multicoloured birds! Strange species of animals and insects! All of them neat and bright! But why are the people here like this? Er ..., I hope you get me. I mean ...'

The Tribal King laughed out loudly. 'The people here are part of the nature you admire. Have you seen any bird or animal brushing their teeth in the morning? Or taking regular baths at fixed times? Which animal washes and changes its clothes?'

Aparna felt like pointing out, *'But animals don't wear clothes at all. You wear a loincloth at least!'* She controlled her mischief and stayed silent. Pradip Lahiri and Bejoy Luxmi were moving towards them. The Tribal King raised his hand. 'Don't come. Stay where you are.'

They froze on the spot at the fierce tone of authority in his voice.

Kashyap looked at Neela Kalyani, sitting at the distance. He felt irritated at Pradip Lahiri for leaving her there all alone. Aparna felt the latent fear in him that some Ravana may steal his Seetha if left alone. Seeing Kashyap's attention diverted, Aparna felt obliged to move the conversation forward.

'Is it true that everything has to be offered to you first?'

His eyes started burning. 'Yes, it is true. What is that to you? I know where you are heading.'

'No offence meant, Sir,' Aparna smiled benignly at him. 'A set of people who stubbornly resist all social and moral codes ... I mean, progress. That was the impression given to us about the life here.'

'I don't know your language. I am not interested in hearing it either. Get out of here ... fast!'

Bejoy Luxmi said in English, 'How can he behave like this after taking money from us? He is not the king, he is the Satan.'

The man jumped up from the cot. Aparna saw that he was tall and muscular and had an attractive figure, though not clean.

'I told you I don't want to hear your dirty language. Leave now. Or else none of you will leave this place alive.'

The Guide came running to them and tried to pacify the enraged man, all the while signalling with his eyes to his clients not to say anything.

'I am the law here,' the Tribal King shouted. 'Your right is not my right. Girl, you asked a good question. Yes, everything is offered to me first. I enjoy everything first—be it girls, fruits or flowers. Want to know anything else?'

Women of different ages came out of the huts at the noise. Aparna saw that they were all at different stages of pregnancy. Some looked as if ready to give birth at the next moment; some in the budding stage of the child inside, some looking tired with protruded bellies.

'Get lost, all of you,' he thundered.

Neela Kalyani sprang up at the terrible voice. Kashyap ran to her immediately.

'Let us go,' he said. 'Neela is not at all well.'

'Yes, let us go; that is better,' said the Guide.

Their walk back was really fast, though they were not conscious about it.

'Hey you, Guide,' Bejoy Luxmi raised her voice. 'Did you really give all that money to that dirty man? We don't trust you at all. You made us take an appointment to meet that dirty scoundrel as though he were a celebrity; yet he refused to cooperate with us. Why? I want to know why. You cheated us.'

'Lux, leave him alone,' said Pradip. 'We have to be blamed for setting out with this nincompoop hoping to get an exclusive story.'

The drummer saw them and started walking behind them again beating loudly on the drum. It was loud enough to pierce anyone's ear drums. Soon a batch of dirty urchins joined him and they started their pranks. The dirtiest of them tried to pull away the shawl from around Aparna's shoulders.

'What do you think you are doing?' Aparna turned to him with lightning in her eyes.

'Madam, please ... don't say anything. Dangerous,' the Guide looked really worried. 'Please walk fast.'

Another topless boy jumped from behind and grabbed the expensive hair clip from Neela Kalyani's hair. The hair came tumbling down around her face and she turned to him with a fierce glare.

'*Saab*, please give some money to the drummer,' the Guide requested. 'He will go away then, with his mob. Otherwise they would keep on disturbing the ladies.'

A man sitting on the street-side playing cards, shouted something at the drummer and the drummer laughed aloud, looking at the women.

The Guide said, 'Look, he has passed an obscene comment on the ladies. He has told the drummer to share with him whatever he gets. *Saab*, I will not be able to lead you out safely if this continues. Please throw some money at them.' The Guide seemed to change colour with fear.

'Go to hell,' said Pradip and threw some currency at the crowd. As the boys and the drummer ran after them, the Guide said, 'Good. Now let us move fast.'

'Are all these kids born of the tribal king?' Neela Kalyani asked the Guide.

'Well, need not necessarily be,' The Guide said. 'It is a must that he has to break the virginity—of all the girls of the tribe, including his own daughters. Then, if he is not interested, anyone can take them over.'

'But, these people look so well-fed though they live in dirt and lust. Where do they get the money from—the money for food, drinks, and grass?'

'I'm not sure of that Madam.'

'Don't you remember Apu, what we read about them—that they give asylum to even criminals? Who knows, may be to terrorists too,' Kashyap said. 'Anyway it is damn sure that it is tainted currency that they lavish on drinks and drugs. But that is not my problem. How will we work on the project? And we thought the best one would be ours!'

'We will make something out of all this,' Aparna consoled him. 'You used to tell us that if Goddess Saraswathi is on the pen we can do wonders.'

'Ha ha ha. That is the belief in our *judka* (horse-carriage) street.'

Bejoy Luxmi turned her head away in scorn at the mention of the *judka* street. She could never bring herself to like the common man, though he be her academic friend.

As she walked, Aparna focused on the Tribal King keeping an eye on the fruits and the girls around, watching them to mature. The girl children standing with protruding bellies, pain and fear writ large on their eyes. Women with no space of their own. Women who do not believe in complaints and protests.

She had to admit that the Tribal King was fiercely handsome. A sort of burning fire. She wished he were a bit clean. If only he had cut his hair and shampooed it , removed the facial hairs, cut his nails, had a bath rubbing off the dirt on his skin ... May be then he would be more handsome than even Kashyap.

His eyes with burning fire in them came to her mind. When he jumped up from the cot in anger, his muscles had become firmer. Aparna's mind shivered a bit, but suddenly she withdrew it from the thought and lapsed into a guilty conscience.

When they reached the city, there were no vehicles around. All the shops were closed. Like an unexpected torrential downpour, a hartal had been declared!

But why? What had happened?

One of the pedestrians, walking fast to reach home, answered their question:

The dead bodies of two raped women had been thrown out of a transport bus into the heart of the city.

'What is new about it?' Pradip Lahiri mumbled in an undertone.

Chapter 2

When Experiences Come Hunting

'Those raped girls do not allow me to sleep in peace, Kashyap,' said Aparna. 'Let us know more about them.'

'Why should we?' Kashyap was evidently annoyed. 'Dead bodies of raped women are being strewn in every part of India almost every day. The loud protest over one lasts only till another body is found. To tell you the truth Apu, I have started losing my faith in God as well as man's goodness.'

'In God too?'

'Yes. I read a book by Richard Dawkins recently. He says that we use the idea of a god to fill a gap in the brain. God is more a psychological need of man—a friend, a father, an elder brother, who exists only in the imagination. Dawkins is of the view that we should find something else to fill in this gap—that is, science, art, friendship with other humans, something like that. This life should be more than a preparation for a life supposed to be there after death. One should fall in love with this life itself. Don't you think it is an excellent idea?'

'So you have become a postmodern rebel of philosophy.'

'No, no, not like that. Dawkins is not a philosopher; he is a biologist. I just read him out of curiosity.'

Aparna always had great respect for Kashyap's boundless, encyclopedic knowledge. Pradip too was a man of reading, but he could never claim such a vast kingdom of knowledge as his own.

'So let us fall in love with the present, forget everything else, and live on, ok? Only two more semesters to go; then we will get our degrees, perhaps placements too. Life begins only after that. So my intelligent friend, my beauty, let us concentrate on our studies now; throw all else into the shade. The press will go after the history of the victims.'

'Intelligence and beauty .... I go slowly on both,' Aparna laughed back at him.

'Exactly what Neela too says,' Kashyap said, joining the laughter. 'But she always fishes for compliments. You know, Neela is not at all like you.'

Aparna had always felt that Kashyap would marry Neela Kalyani in the end. If so, he is also not intelligent enough. Neela Kalyani was like the princess in the Vikramaditya tales whose skin was so sensitive that even moonlight could cause blisters. The one born with the proverbial silver spoon in her mouth. The one who slept lavishly on the feather-bed of luxuries. Kashyap was a self-made man. How could he bring her to his small house in the *judka* street where lived his old father who still made a living by driving the *judka*, his mother who worked as a maid, his two sisters still students. Chances are that he may give them a kick on the back and go with Neela Kalyani to her palace of comforts and riches. Yes, the law of probability tilts more to that possibility.

Kashyap got up, placing his empty tea cup on the table.

'Which way are you going?' Aparna asked him. 'Can you drop me at Mayur Vihar? I have to see our Professor.'

'Of course.'

Kashyap was always a gentleman who would never say 'No' to ladies.

He kick-started his old bike which had been the joke of the campus and they set out.

Flat 8B. On the chiselled piece of wood was written artistically—Dr Umakant Narang. Dr Shachi Narang.

Remembering with a smile the campus joke about the incompatible couple as Shiva living with the wife of Indra, Aparna rang the doorbell.

'Of course,' said Narang. 'Of course rape has a centrifugal effect. In the centre would be the raped girl—the survivor as per modern lingo—and the rapist or rapists. In the first circle around them would be the close family members of them and their lovers, if any. You know, in any study on rape, the rapists are as important as the survivors. The effect of the action would be felt mostly by the first circle of close kith and kin. In the second circle around the first circle we can place the other relatives, friends and even the neighbours. Their additions and deletions to the story enhance the fancy element. The third circle would be around them comprising people who read about it, people who crowd to see them, people who delight in hearsay, etc. Their contribution will take us away from the centre and change the story, unbelievably perhaps. Like that the circles spread out far and wide like ripples.'

Umakant Narang drew circles on the paper to substantiate his words. In the centre of the circles, he had drawn unskillfully the outline of a girl's body with a man standing astride. He seemed to be absorbed in his thoughts as he spoke again:

'And the interesting factor is that, the centre-action would affect even the people in the outermost circle. Sometimes it would affect a stranger in the outermost circle more than anyone in the first circle. It has happened.'

'Yes Sir; that is my theory,' Aparna said. 'The butterfly effect of rape.'

'Long before you people came, there was a smart and intelligent boy in the campus—Ujwal. His performance record in the university is yet to be broken. He got a highly paid job in the *New York Times.* I met him years later on one of my trips to New York. Bachelor still, though with salt and pepper hair. He opened up in his flat after a few drinks. When he was a child, there was an obnoxious rape somewhere far off which the press had highlighted and which was discussed by every family including his. A grandfather said in anger that the penis of the rapist should be cut off and thrown to the waves. Ujwal remembers how he stood shivering behind a half-closed door, listening to the words, and holding on to his penis for fear of castration. Whenever he had looked at his penis after that, he had a guilty feeling as though he were also part of the tragedy. It had affected his sexual prowess. He had girlfriends, but could not satisfy any. He was leading a solitary life in his middle-age—with only platonic relationships and the resultant frustration.'

Professor Narang sat thoughtfully for a while, went inside the room and returned with a newspaper.

'Aparna, have a look at this,' he said, pointing out a matrimonial advertisement.

Fair girl. Beautiful. 25 years. Believes that marriage is only friendship, not sex. Interested people may contact. No preference of caste, creed, age or finance.

'Where does this girl stand, in your opinion?' Narang asked. 'In the centre, or in one of the peripheral circles?'

'Why should she be anywhere there?' Aparna asked. 'Should we theorize on the hypothesis that she might be a raped girl or one affected by the sight or hearsay about rape? To me it appears a matter of personal choice.'

'Well, that would be the answer if you oversimplify. But a student with a research bent of mind should not yield to such easy conclusions. Curiosity is a virtue. So is imagination. Especially for a good student.'

Aparna beamed a stupid smile. She remembered the Tribal King, the female bodies that he enjoyed with a strange rightfulness, his semen turning to babies in their uteruses. The butterfly flaps its wings. The effect spreads from the centre to the whole country. Bleeding women are thrown out of buses. Thrown from the ships to the waves. At the centre stands he—, the Tribal King with fire in his eyes, a powerful metaphor.

'Rape always had a centre of patriarchy,' said Narang. 'The only place where man's absolute authority could not be brought down by the feminine force. She can be equal in all other fields; she can even surpass him in some of them, but not in this field.'

Was there a latent pride in Narang's voice? Aparna looked closely at him and he smiled. Aparna wanted to tell him that she disagreed with him. She remembered reading about a notorious rapist being fed on Viagra by a group of women, and raped brutally by them. What one cannot do alone, one can do standing united. But she knew Narang would not accept hearsay; he needed substantiation for everything. So, leaving that topic, she told him: 'I plan to proceed with my argument, taking the Tribal King as the metaphor for patriarchal authority. He sees all the female bodies as offerings to him—be they that of mother, wife, daughter or anyone in the tribe. Yet he is adored by the women. Feared and respected by the menfolk. Protected by them all.'

'Has he affected you so much, Aparna? There is a wild glint in your eyes whenever you speak of him. I remember the emotional fervour with which you talked about him in the class seminar.'

'True Sir, he follows me like madness. I just want to get him out of my system by writing. You know, writing him off—words can be means of exorcism.'

He noticed that her voice trembled as she spoke.

'You showed his photograph in the seminar presentation. But I have forgotten his face.'

'His photos are here in my tablet,' Aparna said with excitement. 'Pradip had secretly taken some photographs with his hidden button-camera. I had copied some from there. And, fortunately, I have my tablet with me now.'

As she was searching for the tablet in her bag, Narang sat looking at her curiously. A typical South Indian beauty. Long hair and chubby cheeks. Some girls feel irresistibly attracted to rapists, a sort of aberration. Are Aparna's excitement and rage caused by some such wild feeling?

Aparna showed Narang the photo of the Tribal King. Eyes red with intoxication. Drinks or drugs? Unkempt hair scattered on the forehead and the shoulders. Strong ebony-dark body. Loincloth that does not do its function properly.

'He is really handsome,' said Narang. 'But you have to scrub him clean first.' He had a sinister smile on his eyes and lips.

'Yes Sir. Look at the intense look in his eyes. Piercing, no? As if he can look beyond your mind. Hypnotizing look. How old does he look Sir?'

'Well I can only guess. I think between 55 and 60.'

'Oh? I thought he would be somewhere between 45 and 50.'

'That is where I am,' said Narang, gently drawing Aparna to him. 'Between 45 and 50. Is that your favourite age for men, Aparna?'

Aparna wondered why she was not resisting his advances.

'I have always thought of your five-member gang,' said Narang. 'Number five is the problem. Had it been four, I could say who belonged to whom. But three women and two men is a conundrum. Whom do you like best Aparna—Kashyap or Pradip?'

Aparna was silent. She noticed that Narang's voice was faltering and his lips were twitching uncontrollably. Foreplay is really a matter of art. When the man unbuttons his shirt, the forest of chest hair revealed will emit magical waves that would make the woman's eyes go sleepy.

'Do my eyes have his intensity, Aparna?' Narang asked.

His flat turned into a forest and darkness descended on it. The Tribal King sat on his cot, surrounded by women pregnant and not, laughing out loud.

Chapter 3

The Other

'Have you noticed Aparna's recent change?' asked Neela Kalyani. 'Her laugh has become so artificial. Language is artificial. Behaviour more so.'

Four members of the gang, except Aparna, had gathered in Pradip Lahiri's room. They are going to watch a short movie titled *The Other*—a joint project of Pradip and Bejoy Luxmi. They have tried to project the Other in all individual beings. In fact, both of them had spent the whole of the previous night in Lahiri's room to do the editing and dubbing. Kashyap and Neela Kalyani had helped in the daytime, but Aparna had been staying away for the past two days on the excuse of migraine, her family-gift.

'It is her mood-swing,' said Bejoy Luxmi. 'Don't we know that she is always swinging from one mood to another?'

'Yesterday something happened,' said Kashyap suddenly. 'In fact I wanted to tell you about it, but somehow it just skipped my mind. You remember, I could not join you people for lunch as I had to go out to buy batteries for my camera? When I went alone to the canteen to grab some food before class, it was almost empty. To my surprise I found Aparna sitting alone at a table. With two burgers and a Pepsi in hand, I hurried to her. Believe me friends, I was terrified. She had so strange a look on her face. She had a sandwich on her plate which was cut into mustard-size pieces and she was scattering them on the table with her fork. The look on her eyes was so fierce and intense, as if she was cutting a person to pieces and scattering the pieces around. What an intense look! With gritted teeth and tightened facial muscles. I was really scared.'

'Ha ha ha ha. The Other,' Pradip Lahiri laughed loudly.

'Shut that crap Pradip!' Neela Kalyani shouted at him. 'Tell me Kashyap, then what happened?'

'I asked her, Apu, what is this? What do you think you are doing? She raised her eyes. They had a strange look in them. A murderer's eyes. But slowly the look melted and Aparna relaxed. She smiled at me with a "Hi Kashyap". But the one minute she took to come back to herself—that really shook me up.'

'Her change frightens me too,' said Bejoy Luxmi. 'Pradip, do you remember the night when you dropped me rather late at the hostel, after our Connaught Place adventure? That night as I sneaked into the hostel, it was so late that all had gone to sleep. The light in the main hall is never switched off. I was carefully stealing in when I saw Aparna rushing down the staircase like a whirlwind. As I stood stunned, she rushed back up with the same speed. With some premonition I hid myself behind the furniture. She rushed down and ran up again.I don't know how many times she did that. Not knowing that she was being watched, she stopped at the foot of the stairs panting like a dog and then slowly went up. She did not come down after that.

I waited for a safe while and then went up the stairs myself. The door to her room was only half-closed. I could hear her sobbing inside.'

After the initial shock, Pradip Lahiri became annoyed. 'Why didn't you tell us all this earlier?'

'We may be friends, but we still have to respect each other's privacy.'

'That is a lame excuse.'

'What would you have done, had I told you? You can't confront her and ask why she behaved like that. Can you imagine how she would react to it?'

Kashyap intervened. 'Till I saw her weird behaviour in the canteen I never thought she had any problem. But Luxmi, you could have told us about the staircase incident. We would have helped her in some way. Even now it is not late.'

'I wonder why I never noticed all this,' said Pradip Lahiri. 'Guess I was full of *The Other*. When did I see her last? Yes, two days back. Do you remember Lux, the peepul trunk in the movie where you can see an indistinct human face—the loaded image we have used? It was Aparna who suggested it. She said a friend from her Kerala college days had sent her such an image. She searched her mailbox, found it and forwarded it to me. Neela and Kashyap, it is the image that Lux likes most in the movie. You can see the movie in a minute, friends. The girl comes running and collapses under a tree. The camera zooms on the trunk and the indistinct human face becomes clear. Aparna was perfectly normal when she made that suggestion. She told me that it would convey a two-fold message: one, such invisible faces are there in nature offering refuge to the victims, and two, invisible forces are keeping a watch on the criminals.'

'How many good suggestions had I made?' Bejoy Luxmi feigned sadness. 'You don't even remember them. But you remember Apu's words.'

Kashyap detected a tint of jealousy in her voice.

'Come on Lux,' Lahiri put his hands round her shoulders. 'Don't you forget that this is our joint effort? Should we thank each other? Are we so distant?'

'You are always being watched! I like that,' Kashyap said. 'With so many hidden cameras around, it sounds terribly true.'

Bejoy Luxmi laughed. 'Pradip has a camera even on the button of his shirt. Don't you remember, he took pictures of that dirty tribal ruler with that.'

'That was really something!' Pradip laughed. 'He won't even let us go near. But no one suspected. It would have been another story had we been caught!'

'Or, no story left to be told.'

'Dirty place and dirty people!' Neela Kalyani expressed disgust. 'Hell on the earth. Who else but you would want their photographs?'

'Thousands of people saw them on my blog and read about them. Haven't I showed you their comments? The print media took my matter and published it. It led to feminist revolts in the campus and outside. Yet how can you talk like this?'

'Who watches us now?' Bejoy Luxmi smiled. 'Now—at this minute?'

'Big Brother is watching you. Don't you remember Orwell?' Kashyap got up and pretended to be the Big Brother. 'I am watching you. Your computer and mobile are all under my surveillance.'

'Yes, true. There is someone in the computer, watching me,' said Neela Kalyani. 'When I begin writing to my schoolmate

Sandhya, "Dear Sandhya," the computer will ask "Sandy?" It cannot understand that my friend is Sandhya and will try to impose a western name.'

'When you see my movie, you will understand it,' said Pradip. 'There is a scene where the girl writes a letter to the government. She begins with 'Respected' and writes the Governor's name. The computer, failing to grasp the Indian name comes up with other suggestions. Some of the names it suggests are really funny.'

Pradip started laughing.

Luxmi stopped him. 'You idiot, please don't break the suspense. I wonder why Aparna is late. Will she not come at all? If so, we should begin the movie before Pradip spills out all the beans.'

'I will call her,' Neela Kalyani pressed Aparna's number. 'Hey Apu, where the hell are you? We are all waiting for you... No we haven't started. Ok, ok, hurry up.'

'She has almost reached,' Neela informed her friends.

'How did her voice sound?' Kashyap's anxiety was evident. 'Was she happy, or ...?'

'Brimming with happiness,' Neela Kalyani laughed.

'Come, Kashyap,' Pradip got up. 'Let's go to the vending machine and get some chips. You girls take care of the beer. Lux, hope you will remember, on the rocks for me.'

Neela smelled the two glasses on the table. Moist with the previous night's beer, they emitted a sweet and sour smell like tamarind. Neela put on a wry expression and said, 'These men!' When she picked up the glasses and went to wash them, Bejoy Luxmi suppressed her sly smile. Who knows better than her that it was not two men, but one man and one woman? She lit a cigarette and sat back leaning on the chair comfortably.

When they came back with sachets of fries, Kashyap and Pradip were laughing hilariously.

'Girls, here is the latest bulletin,' Pradip said. 'We saw Sonjay Mithra outside.'

Bejoy Luxmi was pushing the books and CDs on the table to one side to make place for the beer glasses. She said with a smirk, 'If it is about that bookworm, we don't want to hear the latest bulletin.'

'Sonjay! Bookworm!' The men thumped each other on the back and laughed.

'Stop guffawing,' Neela Kalyani became angry. 'Sonjay lives in this hostel. So what is new about meeting him here?'

'Do you know where we met him?'

'Where? Tell us.'

'Guess!'

'Pradeeeeeep, don't try my patience too far.'

'Ok. Your bookworm was at the condom-vending machine.'

'You should have seen his face when he saw us!'

'And the way he rushed off towards his room! Ha ha ha.'

Now the girls became silent. They always had respect for Sonjay, the boy who concentrated only on his studies, performed well in class, who openly shared his dream to enter the administrative service.

'Sanyasi-turned fox!' Pradip laughed loudly again.

'But who is the girl in his room?' The girls looked at each other.

'Can be anyone,' Kashyap answered. 'He is fair and handsome; girls must be chasing him. Only thing is, we never suspected him.'

'It must be Nileena,' said Bejoy Luxmi on a sudden inspiration. 'Nileena had a crush on him from the very beginning.'

'Crush? On that stupid nerd?' Neela Kalyani could not believe it. 'No, Luxmi, not Nileena anyway. She is more sensible. I think it must be our Constance Ruth. She also has IAS dreams.'

'But Sonjay ... of all the people in the campus!'

'The Other!' Pradip laughed again.

And then the door opened and Aparna entered the room, closing the door behind her. She was full of energy and extremely cheerful. Placing her bag on the bookshelf, she came, all smiles, to sit near Neela Kalyani on the bed. Apologizing for the delay caused by her, she extended her hand towards the beer glass offered.

'But what happened Apu?' Neela asked. 'Did you forget about our meeting?'

'No, no. I had come half-way, but then I had to go back.'

'Why?'

Aparna whispered in her ear, 'Scarlet Pimpernel.* Much delayed this time, but came unexpectedly.' Aparna laughed in a weird manner and drank the beer.

---

* Scarlet Pimpernel: A red flower. Girls use it as code for their menstruation. The novel of this name written by Baroness Emmuska Orczy is well-known.

Interval-II

Kamala-3

When the train stopped at a station, Govind asked Kamala, 'I'm going to buy food. Shall I buy some for you too?'

'No, thanks,' said Kamala and placed her book on the seat. She sat thinking about Aparna. Aparna was living in a city that allows all freedom to girls, and she has male friends too. Yet how can she worry herself to death about delayed menstruation just because she had sex with a man? Quite unbelievable! That too in the metro where Umakant Narangs brew like mosquitoes, tribal kings become heads of houses and open relationships thrive. Recognized condom-vending machines are instituted for students. *The only way to get rid of a temptation is to yield to it*—Oscar Wilde's idea seems to be shared by the authority. In such a world how can a student be so obsessed with a mere episode of love-making? Let us say that Narang attacked her quite unexpectedly. Couldn't Aparna just walk to a medical shop nearby and buy a pill that would have liberated her?

The Southerners in the campus boast that in their corner of the world, moral values have not totally dried up. Now, is that the real problem of Aparna? But Kamala too belongs to South India. How can Aparna have all this agitation and consternation that Kamala never had at the first time? A veteran that she is now, Kamala could not follow the workings of Aparna's mind.

Their five-member gang is like Kamala's Fourcentric gang, though not as progressive. Kamala laughed at Narang's words, '*Number five is the problem. Had it been four, I could say who belonged to whom. But three women and two men is a conundrum.*' Let him visit the Fourcentric group—two men and two women only; and let him say who is whose. He will never be able to guess the truth. The Fourcentric gang has started with clear guidelines—firm in the resolve that the green-eyed monster would never be allowed in.

But of late Kamala had started to feel certain premonitions whether the resolve is getting relaxed. Once Sidan had told her, 'Hey Kamu, don't laugh at me, but I feel like marrying you. You are my girl.' For days she had been disturbed as she never wanted to be the causative agent for the gang's fall. She could not dismiss it as a mere joke. But Vinayak and Devangi laughed aloud on hearing it, confusing Kamala all the more.

Mrinalini Madam, in her class on Evolutionary Philosophy, had said, '*Mangalasutra* is only dead metal. If that metal were to come alive, there should be the throbbing of a culture behind it. Unfortunately today's generation is indifferent to it.'

While saying that, Mrinalini Madam looked slyly at Kamala and Deva. Both of them sat straight-backed and returned her cautious glances with a bold stare. They abhorred dead metals as well as the status of the wife. All they needed, all they cared for, was freedom, independence.

Kamala went out to wash her hands, came back and opened her food packet. She saw that Amma had packed chapatti and vegetable curry. And that means she had packed puris as breakfast for tomorrow. That is Amma's systematic way.

The couple had started eating their food. Kamala saw that they never looked at or talked to each other. Will the words fly away at one stage from every marriage? Kamala's mother also is rather quiet; her father is not quite eager to talk to his wife. So it must be a general case. Will it happen in the case of friendships too? Maybe not, as there is no chair of authority in such relationships. So we are safe, Kamala smiled to herself.

Govind has not returned to his seat. Impulsively she leaned and took *The Selfish Gene*, the book he had been reading. She was surprised to note that the author was Richard Dawkins, the name she just read in the novel! She placed the book back and continued eating as Govind walked in.

She thought of the intricate structure of the female mind. The first wound on the female body will affect the mind. In fact the wound on the woman's mind will never heal though she becomes wife, mother and grandmother. Suppose the first wound was inflicted without the support of love, the trauma would be more horrendous. How will the raped survivors see their body after their suffering? Kamala's first experience was not out of love, but it was not rape either. She had gone to the hostel room of a male friend for combined study, just in the hostel way. It was then that she saw condoms as well as the condom vending machine in the premises of the hostel. After post-graduation that friend left the campus for good. He was never interested in research and settled down when he got a post in a bank. They mailed each other for some time; as mail after mail proceeded, she saw romance drying up slowly and the last mail she got had an attachment – an invitation for his marriage.

Devangi's life was not as simple as that. Her body was insulted when she was just 10 years old. Even now she carries the shattering blow within her. She has told Kamala that during intercourse she would tightly close her eyes and keep them closed till it is over.

'Would you like water?' Govind asked her. In answer she raised her water bottle brought from home and he just smiled. He is better than the self-obsessed couple. Though he reads *The Selfish Gene,* he is not selfish at all.

As she finished her chapattis, Vinayak's phone call came for her. 'Kamu, what is the time of your arrival? Do you want me to come to the station?'

Vinayak can speak only in a high-pitched voice. It will invite other listeners sitting nearby. Kamala glanced at Govind to see if the sound reaches him.

'No, don't bother please. I will reach safely.'

'Deva arrives at 4 in the morning. I am going to pick her. We can while away our time till your train reaches, or, if you are the first to arrive, we can wait for Deva.'

'No Vinu, thanks. My train is running late.'

'Ok, but don't create a scene here saying, "No one cares for me."'

'Who makes scenes usually—Deva or I? Don't confuse us please.'

'Ok, leave it. Come fast. Waiting restlessly. Love you. Umma.'

'Goodnight. Love you.' Kamala looked at Govind and returned the kiss in a low key. '*Why should I bother about this man who is only another passenger,*' she asked herself in annoyance.

Govind was connecting the scattered sound waves that had come to him. He suppressed the impulse to laugh. The man who gave her a kiss first, never talked so loud. So this is someone else. How can a man trust any girl in these times? If the girl one marries happens to be an unkissed virgin, the man would really be lucky.

The two men left the cabin almost together to wash their hands, leaving Kamala alone with the woman.

The woman spoke in haste to Kamala in a low tone: 'Excuse me, can you tell me who wrote that book—the one you are reading now?'

'Chandrika Balan,' Kamala showed her the title page.

'Do you know her?'

'No.'

After a minute of silence, the woman asked, 'She had cancer, right?'

'So I have heard,' said Kamala. 'But I think she is cured now.'

'I have read her articles on cancer. But is cancer curable? Do you think it can be cured?'

'Yes. Doctors say that early detection and the correct medical treatment can cure it completely.'

The woman sat thoughtful. Kamala guessed that she was suffering from cancer; they might be coming to Delhi for treatment. Her heart went out to the woman in sympathy. But the lady said, 'Our daughter—Thara—she is dying. Cancer! She had left home four years back marrying a person from another religion. After that we haven't seen her. We heard news of her becoming a mother. But even then this man did not allow me to go and see her. Now he comes with me—to see her die. What use is sympathy and love if they come rather late?'

She had bitterness in her voice and she kept on looking at the closed door of the cabin even while weeping. Kamala was at a loss as to what to say. Saving her, the husband walked in and sat in his place. The lady returned to the world of stony silence.

All relationships gift only sorrow. That is the reason why the Fourcentrics have decided not to get entangled in relationships. They will live like this as long as health allows. Kamala thought of their saving plan; each would contribute every month and the amount will grow big as they reach old age. That common fund would be spent on building a posh Old Age Home with 20 rooms, four of which would be reserved for the four founders. They have planned their silent exits from there.

But who will bother to understand them? The world has its fixed standards and codes. The daughter dismissed from home because she married a person from outside the family's religion, will be taken back only when she develops some terminal illness like cancer! For the Fourcentrics there is no religion, no offspring, and no parents even, and so no illness will bother anyone else.

Govind went to his upper berth after saying 'Goodnight' to Kamala. As if waiting for him to go, the woman spread the railway sheets and blankets and lay down. Lying comfortably on the lower berth, Kamala opened the novel and resumed reading: **Part III: The Family.**

Part III

The Family

Chapter 1

The Nuptial

In Aparna's place, that is Kerala, mustard and black-coloured dragonflies appear in August-September. Their appearance is a forerunner to the state festival of Onam and they are hailed as *Onathumbis.* Aparna used to wonder where these dragonflies were hiding till the Onam season, also, where they disappear to, after the season. She is now sitting in the garden chair in the front yard of her home, watching the dragonflies fluttering about.

'*One day I will discover your hideout*,' said Aparna to the playful dancing creatures.

'*Really? Then you have to be born as one of us*,' said a mischievous dragonfly.

'*Well, I don't mind*, said Aparna. '*Anyway, your world will not have tears and misery, lust and rape, bastards born of adultery, orphaned kids. I would love to be part of your world*.'

The dragonfly looked at her in a puzzled way, '*I couldn't follow half of what you said, but if by lust you mean sex, it is as dear to us as our lives. Who doesn't enjoy sex, whatever he/she may be?*'

The dragonfly set out to chase another one, when Aparna said, '*Well, you may like sex, but, to us, love is dearer.*'

The dragonfly paused, hovering in the wind, and asked, '*Love? What is love?*'

The other dragonfly, waiting to be chased by this one, said, '*Love is a stupid concept of these human beings; it does not exist. Don't waste time listening to this woman. Are you going to chase me or not? If not, I have to find someone else to chase me.*'

The second dragonfly started moving and the first one made a leap. '*Don't leave me, I'm coming.*'

'*Love is a stupid concept of these human beings!*' Aparna was stung by the words. Where did these dragonflies study? Delhi? Mumbai? Or in Kerala? May be they are right. Hiranmayi Devi had sliced her veins in the classroom itself. She was sitting near Aparna in the class. Blood had squirted out onto Aparna's dress too. Hiranmayi never came to class after that. Discharged from the hospital, she was taken away by her parents. The last sight Aparna had of her was sitting with bowed head between a sad-looking old man and woman. She did not even raise her head to say 'Bye'. But Joen, the culprit, just walked around boldly in the campus. Nothing seemed to have affected him. He still remained the master sportsman of the campus, and, before the course ended, he got a good job too. How many campus examples are there like that! Outside campus too; in fact all over the country.

The dragonflies are luckier. Aparna looked curiously at them dancing away, the drops of sunlight reflecting from their wings. Some of them dance alone; some in pairs. They are free to appear and go away when they like.

On her lap lay a photograph. It was of a young man who had once appeared like an *onathumbi* and disappeared too. She took the photograph and looked it over again. Firm face and friendly smile. He was standing in front of a curtain in a studio, looking at the camera. Evidently a matrimonial photo. It was Aparna's mother who gave her the photograph.

'This is our old way,' said Amma. 'You, the new-gen, like pictures in computers and video-talks.'

'Who brought this?'

'A friend of your father. He is a family friend of the boy. He knows the boy very well; the relatives too. He says we would be lucky if this marriage takes place. They are rich with well-placed relatives; you will never lack in anything. By the way, the boy is an only son; no siblings. One look at the picture and someone whispered from the depths of my mind that this is Aparna's partner for life.'

Whispered from the depths of my mind ... Aparna smiled to herself. Her mother was a lover of literature once; but after her marriage she could never read even a newspaper in full. Fate had chained her to the kitchen. Aparna's father never read anything other than the newspaper; more than that he never could stand anyone wasting time reading books. Yet, Aparna's mother used to buy books slyly with the money sent by her son Deepak. Deepu also used to smuggle in books and periodicals for her whenever he came home. So Amma knew the man in the picture even otherwise.

'He is a poet too,' Amma told her. 'I have read in the newspaper that he has recently received an award for the best young poet. I've seen the photograph also of the award function. You were in Delhi then. But at that time I never thought that a proposal for marriage will come like this.'

Aparna remembered a night in the train. A masculine voice was speaking into a mobile:

Garlands of jasmine fell on the hill of hymens.
The dark and lonely hill, the Virgin Hill.

'They will be coming this Sunday to see you. Alright?' Amma seemed to have a tremor in her voice.

'Let them come,' Aparna smiled.

Amma heaved a sigh of relief and smiled warmly. 'To tell you the truth, your father and I were really worried whether you would bring someone with you from Delhi. Some of our relatives also tried to key us up. I had a dream too that my son-in-law walked in with a turban, beard and a sword. The Sikhs call their sword *kirpan*, no?'

Aparna laughed loudly: 'So you were expecting me to be Aparna Dara Singh?'

When Amma left her alone, she looked fondly at the picture in her hand and whispered, 'Have you recognized me?'

'Have you recognized me?' A few days later the man in the picture asked her directly. He was sitting on a chair in the balcony of *Sauparnika*, Aparna's house. Aparna, sitting on the swing chair near him, was light-heartedly moving to and fro. Happiness shone bright on her face as she looked at him.

'I recognized you the minute I set my eyes on your photo.'

'I'm not as intelligent as you,' he laughed softly. 'I took some time to recognize you. My first impression was, 'Haven't I seen this girl somewhere?' Then slowly memories refreshed themselves. The name Aparna on the railway chart. The serious girl immersed in a book that had a funny name. You were very serious on that day; but from the photograph you smiled at me. I connected at last.'

'It was one year ago, right?'

'No, about two years. But your face used to flash on my mind sometimes.'

'Oh? Yet you needed time to connect. I recognized you the moment I saw the picture.'

'Well ... You were too serious a girl then; now with a bright smile.'

'Don't tell me that you were different. How seriously engaged were you with your laptop!'

'Oh, that was a mere show of self-conceit, to keep strangers away. I would have talked to you earlier but for those two nuisance kids. I remember their funny mother too, who used to yell into her phone.'

Chinnu–Minnu and their Jeans-mom. Aparna smiled to herself. How fresh they have come up in memory after one year. Was it yesterday, she wondered, that they travelled with them?

'Aparna, let me ask you something frankly. Have you ever thought of me after we parted?'

After they parted ... So many things had happened. Life was hectic with positive and negative happenings. Aparna decided to be honest. She said, 'No.'

She saw his face going dim for a second, but there was nothing she could do. She had literally thrown him out of her mind when she got out of the train. Just a fellow passenger! She had never felt anything more!

When he remained silent, looking at some imaginary point in the distance, she knew she had hurt him, though not intentionally. She thought of asking whether he still carried the laptop. But she thought the better of it, for it might worsen the situation. He is extra-sensitive, it is evident; one has to be extra-careful when one deals with poets. So she asked a different question:

'I remember you reciting some lines of your poem on the phone. Have you published your poems?'

Immediately he became zestful. 'Two poems I have published in print media. But it is the social media that is my main venue. After my award—hope you know about it—a publisher has come forward to bring out a collection.'

As he raved on about his poetry Aparna realized that like all the poets she had met in the campus and outside, he is also a self-centered man. She knows from experience that those who talk on are never good listeners. People say that unless one marries a good talker, one's old age would become dull and monotonous. But if the talker would talk only about oneself, wouldn't old age become intolerable?

Aparna sat swinging herself gently, pretending to listen to him, nodding and smiling at the right places. When he became tired of himself, the man decided to come back to Aparna.

'By the way, why didn't you take up the job you got in *Economic Times*?'

'That was campus placement. I just went with the others and got it by fluke. Anyway I had no desire to stay in Delhi any longer.'

'I became more interested in this proposal after hearing that. The way you carried yourself about in the train was disturbing me, as you behaved like a metro girl. The fact that you had studied in Delhi is rather dismissive. But if you give up a good job that everyone hankers after and decide to return to your native land, it shows your attachment to your roots and values.'

A name carved artistically on a wooden piece came to Aparna's mind. The reason why she left Delhi. Umakant Narang. The intellectual professor with the face of a pig. The campus version of the tribal leader.

Aparna, why do you avoid me like this? Come on girl, these things are done every day in this city. Nothing is taboo here. You or I are not the first persons to do it either. The way you look at me is as if I had committed something heinous. Look Aparna dear, sex is the most divine action; no God has talked against it. Sexual discipline is man-made, to preserve the discipline in society. As long as we play without disrupting the master plan of discipline, no harm will come out of it. Come, let us enjoy the last few days.

Aparna had turned away and walked back, her heart and face teeming with contempt for him.

One should cleverly hide the slits in the master plan; if one has intellect enough, one can do it quite easily. When mutilated female bodies are thrown out of the train, they write poems. When small girls die with excessive bleeding and pain as the rapists tear their vaginas with sharp instruments to enjoy themselves, these intellectuals would deliver powerful orations. Over the ripped body of the old woman they will co-ordinate international seminars.

In Delhi, when the ladies suggested the name of Umakant Narang as the inaugurator of the Women's Association, Aparna was the first one to protest. But he was the one who was chosen. He came with Shachi Narang, his wife, who, in the modish way had spread the *pallu* of her sari widely over her left hand. The trailing loose end of the sari displayed heavy golden threadwork and she looked more like a fashion model than a 'normal' Indian woman. She sat on the stage, listening to her husband's words:

'We have to ask ourselves where we have gone wrong. Only the heinous ones can insult the female body that is made to be worshipped high on a pedestal. The woman's body is not created to be merely an object of desire, a source of carnal pleasure. She has been created for a noble end. Adi Shankara's *Saundaryalahari** begins with a statement that without Shakthi, that is, his wife Goddess Parvathi, by his side, Lord Shiva will not be able to do anything. He will not be able even to move. You know, Shakthi means power, strength. A man's power is woman; his strength is his own wife ...'

Professor Shachi Narang smiled proudly at the words and Aparna thought ironically of the man who becomes strong when his strength or Shakthi is not in the vicinity. With a smile of contempt, she had left the hall, without waiting to hear more.

'A penny for your thoughts, Aparna,' said the man sitting near her.

'I was thinking of what you just said—attachment to the roots. What was it that made me leave Delhi for good? Was it the call of the roots, or the call of the unborn flowers and fruits?'

'What do you mean by that? Can you explain it a bit?'

'I don't think it was the call of my roots that made me come back from Delhi. In fact I was ready to go to any part of India other than Delhi. I never wanted to be in Kerala; but I have got stuck here.'

He remembered Aparna's last words to him at the end of the train journey—*I know very well where I want to go and how to get there.* He laughed aloud.

'Did I crack any joke?'Aparna asked. 'What is the meaning of this laughter?'

'No, you didn't. But what you said that day on the Delhi railway platform just popped up; that is all.'

---

* Adi Shankara was one of the greatest philosopher-sages of India. His *Saundaryalahari* which means Waves of Beauty, is a hymn in praise of the Goddess.

'Oh, was that something funny? What did I say?'

'You said, "*I know very well where I want to go and how to get there.*"'

When he threw her own words at her, Aparna was unnerved for a minute. She winced, but tried to cover it up with weak laughter, 'You seem to have a wonderful memory.' She felt that her expression was betraying her nervousness.

'You were the only girl who had talked to me like that. How can I forget it?'

Aparna mumbled softly, 'Sorry,' and he laughed like a victor.

His name was Narendran. Her family members were busy putting invitation letters into envelopes on which was written in embossed golden letters **Aparna Weds Narendran.** Her father insisted that the whole address (without any short forms) should be written on the envelopes to be sent by post and only the name of the head of the family need be written on the envelopes that would be delivered personally.

'But,' Aparna asked, 'Why should we write any name on the invitations that would be delivered personally?'

'Because I want it that way,' said Aparna's father. 'It will give a personal touch.'

'These are antediluvian ideas,' Deepak, Aparna's brother, said. 'Acha, this is the time of email and WhatsApp.'

'Son, my generation may seem antediluvian to you,' said the father, 'but some of us have survived the flood and are tagging on even now. We still believe in the warmth of relationships and emotions. Let them be like that till all of my generation take leave.'

'My handwriting is illegible,' said Deepu. 'Just give me the address book. I will type them all in the computer and take print-outs. We can just cut them and paste them on covers.'

'Sorry, I don't believe in cut-and-paste culture.' The father was irritated. 'My handwriting is quite legible; so I will write them down myself.'

Aparna made a discreet and sly exit. She was also not interested in writing down a hell lot of names and addresses of people whom she did not know. She went to her room and unlocked her laptop. So many mails and cards! She opened the mail of Kashyap first.

Apu, I'm happy in your happiness. I'm sure you will be a good wife and mother. You know, I had always looked upon you with a combo of love and respect. You were modern in every way, but traditional in your ethical values. The ideal match any man would look for. In fact when Neela Kalyani shifted to the US after marriage, I realized my folly. I should have loved you. (He put a smiley of disappointment here) *Apu, I was half-joking, ok? I wish all success to both Narendran and you.*

My life goes on in a better way than I imagined it would. The boss gives me enough money and sucks the juice out of me. But that is expected of their class. Make hay while the sun shines, as the sun may choose to shine upon someone else from tomorrow. Well, I have always loved working. And I am happy to see that my family is improving just because of my hard work. My father does not go to pull rickshaws; I have asked him to rest with proper medication. He has tired himself out to bring us all up; it is time for him to take his well-earned rest. I have also asked my mother not to do the work of housemaid, but she secretly goes to the houses of one or two old customers still. My sisters tell me this, but I'm not supposed to know! Anyway when I go home next, I will ask her to stop it for good ...

Bejoy Luxmi wrote:

Hi Apu, I'm so happy. Pradip and I had a brief discussion now about Narendran and you—whether you loved him, whether that was the reason why you left your attractive job and decided to go back to Kerala. Pradip says that you are a complicated person; a very complex personality. Even I have my doubts whether you will be able to go with the traditional concept of a woman. I really hope and pray that Narendran understands you well.

Here, Pradip and I enjoy our lives and jobs. We haven't yet thought of a marriage; a marriage was never on our agenda, as you very well know. That is only a formality which we can have anytime we want. That is, IF WE EVER WANT IT. Maybe we will get married after I become pregnant. Hahaha.

Under her mail was a post script: *My dearest Apu, all the very best to you. Your dear Pradip.*

Aparna went happily through all the mails and felicitations till she reached a mail from umakantnarang@ gmail.com

One of the teachers told me that you are going to get married. So you see me as a person who does not deserve even an invitation for your marriage. Well, it doesn't matter. But I must tell you this. I never thought you were a virgin, what with your five-member gang and all. Imagine my shock when I discovered it while trying to enter—rather too late. If only you had told me earlier, none of this would have happened.

Let me also share a very personal secret. You were the first virgin I entered. I hope you understand what I mean by it.

A shudder running through her body, Aparna's finger went to the 'Delete' button without reading the mail in full. She was not herself for quite some time.

Then Aparna went to visit Narendran's blog. She read his latest entry posted a few hours ago.

I know now that life is full of strange coincidences. A face that I had seen in a train journey two years back. A serious countenance concentrating on an intellectual book. One who smirks at a comedy film like Turner and Hooch. *I had been drawn to her in spite of myself; but, like all fellow passengers in a train we had to part with a formal bye. Two years ... a long time. She kept playing hide and seek in my memory all the while. And now she is going to enter my life as bride. Here is my first poem to her, written immediately after my visit to her house to see the bride-to-be:*

I never thought I would see you again someday,
That you would be mine one day.
In the solitary cabin with the blue light,
You looked a fairy behind a blue veil.
How could I dream then that one day,
Your face would be mine,
For me to fondle, kiss,
Hold in my hands like a lotus.
My dear, lock me forever in your bright eyes,
As you did on that fateful day,
And I will lock you in mine,
Let's stay as each other's prisoner,
Forever and ever.

The entry had already gained 110 Likes and 37 Comments. Aparna wanted to make her comment too. She wrote:

Cloying romanticism! Utterly disgusting!

She looked at the comment, laughed softly and deleted it.

Chapter 2

Nights of the Poet

Aparna sat speculating on her new role with the new name—Aparna Narendran. Aparna Narendran is not bad; in fact better than Aparna Kashyap Shah or Aparna Pradip Lahiri. She tried various formulations—Aparna Kashyap, Aparna Shah, Aparna Pradip, and Aparna Lahiri. Then she tried jotting her name on the paper adding each of the men she knew in the campus as her surname, except of course one. Aparna Narendran stood two feet above them all. As she tore the paper and put it in the wastepaper basket in the corner, she heard the door opening. It was Narendran in his golden *dhoti* and shirt.

One of the words of advice Aparna's mother had given her was never to do any initial thing that Aparna will not be able to do forever. Taking it literally, Aparna did not get up to receive Narendran. She just sat on the bed, smiling at him. Narendran felt uncomfortable but he concealed it and went towards her. He stopped midway and asked in surprise, 'Oh, you have changed your dress?'

Aparna was sent to the bridal chamber in her silk sari with golden thread-work and she waited for Narendran for a reasonable time. But he took a longer time than she expected, and she was sweating with the heavy sari and ornaments. So she had decided to change into a lighter dress. Narendran looked at her flowing gown with distaste. Aparna felt instinctively that she was falling short of his ideal and said in a subdued tone, 'I will change back if you desire so.'

'It is alright,' said Narendran, evidently happy at her willingness to oblige. He also noticed with pleasure that though she had removed all other ornaments, she had not removed the chain he put round her neck; it was a thick golden chain weighing ten sovereigns. Along with the *mangalasutra* the heavy chain curled round her neck, giving her an added glow.

Narendran sat near her on the bed and stretched his right hand to her. 'Congratulations.'

Aparna also stretched her hand and touched his, saying 'Thanks. Congratulations to you too.'

'Oh, it is not for that. What a surprise it must have been for you to get the appointment order for a job on the previous day of our marriage.'Narendran said with a soft smile. 'When you told me of the interview, I knew then itself that you would do well and get the job. You will bring laurels to that news channel.'

Aparna felt happy to hear it. Narendran moved closer to her and took her hand. Aparna felt a tremor of pleasure running through her body. The serpentine touch of Narang's hands that crept up her neck came to her mind for a second, but she closed the door against it. How soft, how warm Narendran's touch is, she thought. In this warmth I will be able to forget myself and curl up in the world of safety and love.

Narendran said, 'It seems we bring luck to each other. See you have got a job, a good salaried one with enough perks. As for me, do you remember the publisher I told you about the other day? He has sent the contract. I deliberately resisted telling you earlier as I wanted to spring it on you as a pleasant surprise. I will show you the contract now.'

He got up from the bed, opened the table's drawer and took out four large sheets of paper. Looking at them with self-pride, he put them in Aparna's hands.

'Please read it now.'

We accept for publication the collection of poems entitled RESONANCES: LOVE AND DEATH by Narendran P.R. under the following terms...

No.1. The copyright of the poems in this collection rests wholly with ...

As Aparna turned the pages casually, Narendran said with sternness, 'Don't go that fast. Read it carefully. I want you to go through each sentence, taking time. We don't know where a loophole might be hidden. In today's world nobody can be blindly trusted, even if it is a publisher who has approached the writer.'

Would any other woman have gone through a publisher's contract on the first night? Aparna smiled to herself. She felt the charm draining away from the room decorated with flowers. Darting a glance at Narendran she found that he was full of the publisher, not his newly wedded bride. Was this the same person, she asked herself, who sat with sternness of expression in the railway coach, without taking his eyes off the laptop? Again a campus memory came to her mind—*The Other*, a movie by Pradip Lahiri.

Aparna had always felt drawn to men with serious expressions. Even as a child she had felt only repulsion towards men who talked much and who laughed, opening their mouths too wide. There were many such disgusting people in the circle of her father's friends. She had always avoided them, refusing even to serve them tea. She could feel affinity only to Abram Uncle who never talked unnecessarily, who never guffawed. Abram Uncle had never asked little Aparna to sing or dance. Smiles came very rarely to his lips. If he ever smiled at some prank of hers, Aparna used to repeat it to watch him smile again.

Maybe her concept of the ideal man started from Abram Uncle. Serious. Quiet. Handsome. Sharp features.

'See this clause. He is asking for the video rights and translation rights.'

Narendran's breath fell under her ears. She raised her head with goosebumps and looked at him, but he was all absorbed in the contract. Aparna recoiled with self-contempt.

'I wonder if this clause would affect me adversely in future,' Narendran said, his eyes glued to the paper. 'What do you feel Aparna?'

She could not tell him that she was feeling bored; so she asked him, 'How can there be any adverse effect later?'

'That is, suppose we are not able to do anything later? Imagine somebody wants to translate my poems or make a video of them. I have to get the concurrence of the publisher first. And the publisher can refuse permission. Then court ... litigation ... I have no time for all those.'

Aparna suppressed her laughter. As if people would queue up to make movies out of his poems or translate them into all world languages. This must be what is termed the writer's pride. And that too, only a beginner!

'Well, I suggest that you tell the publisher that you cannot agree to certain clauses in the contract. Let us see how he responds and we will decide on our course of action.'

'That is a good suggestion. I will do that,' Narendran carefully put the contract back into the envelope and put the envelope back into the drawer of the table. Then he asked with a mild fear, 'If I ask that, do you think the publisher will cancel the contract?'

'No,' said Aparna. 'You never went in search of him; he was the one who came looking for you.'

'That is right,' Narendran smiled with relief. 'I wanted a wife with intellect and practical wisdom. I really feel blessed that you have come to my life, Aparna.'

Aparna smiled, whispering to herself, *'May he not eat his words in future!'*

Narendran came to her, his face beaming with happiness. 'So Aparna, let us begin our first night. Take the glass of milk from the table and give it to me. Let us not break any ritual.'

The laptop, sitting quietly near the glass of milk and the bowl of fruits on the table, winked at her, as if asking, *'Do you remember me?'*

The man stared at the full breasts of the woman in disbelief. How rich and gargantuan! How soft and massive! Narendran's hands were trembling as they travelled through the heights and depths of his newly discovered country. The curiosity and the enthusiasm of the explorer. As his quivering lips and fingers roamed over her body, Aparna faltered. He is not the pig-faced Narang who had left middle age behind. Narang's movements were soft and tender. He knew how to do it. Patting her body all the way softly with no hurry at all, with a sort of paternal affection ... lulling her senses ... making her fall into a state of not being fully awake, not being fully asleep ... making her body rise to him spontaneously. The ripples he sowed on her body were quite natural and easy, bearing the evidence of an experienced lover. But Narendran's, she felt, was the wild zeal of an immature person. Overindulgence of emotions disfiguring his face and body. Lack of previous experience was evident in his movements.

Lack of previous experience! Aparna literally froze with self-contempt.

But Narendran was too excited to notice it. Kisses with quivering lips. Trembling hands scratching the body and hurting it. The breath that comes down heavily. Finally when he tried to enter her, Aparna yelled with affected pain, mumbling, 'Don't. It hurts. Please don't.'

She had really cried like this in the flat in Mayur Vihar too. But then, it was sincere. Truthful.

After the incomplete sex, Narendran hugged her with a sense of guilt. 'Sorry darling. I didn't want to hurry things up; but somehow, I was too excited and lost control of myself. I'm really sorry. Did I hurt you too much? Do you have pain?'

Aparna was too emotional to answer him. She got up from the bed and rushed to the toilet, banging the door behind her. In the privacy she let go her tears.

Sorry, Narendran. You really deserve a better woman.

Neela Kalyani wrote from San Francisco:

Apu, how is your married life? I remember you telling me that Narendran is a poet. Means he is also a lunatic like you. You know, poet, lover and lunatic—the Shakespeare combo! So you two will be one of the most compatible couples. Ha ha ha. Tell me, how is your job? Since the both of us don't know Malayalam, we don't watch Malayalam channels. But if you will inform me about any special programme of yours, I will try to see it.

We are doing very well here. Utham is a good husband—sensible, loving and so full of fresh ideas. But to tell you the truth, I have started feeling bored. Nowadays I brood on our Delhi days – perhaps a little too much. The spring season of our lives. To be honest, I think of Kashyap a lot. Do you know where Kashyap is? Do you still keep in touch with him? Can you please tell me where he is? Apu, you may think it strange—that I ask about Kashyap after giving him up to marry Utham. But you must understand that it was not easy for me then to take a decision. I was forced by my family into marrying him. They were too practical for me. The class difference, poverty, illiterate relatives ... oh, they had too many things against Kashyap. Finally I felt that what they say would matter in the long run. It was a weak moment for me. I regret it now.

Now Kashyap does not even reply to my mails. I think I have hurt him deeply. But I had no other alternative. Apu, can you help me? Can you please talk to him on my behalf?

Aparna did not respond to Neela Kalyani's mail. She did not want to tell her that Kashyap has given up his former mobile number and mail Id. She did not want to give her the new number and Id. Why should she? How could Neela Kalyani talk so casually about the wound that she had inflicted on Kashyap? Aparna had seen the bleeding wound in his confessional mails. But Kashyap got over it sooner than expected and turned a new leaf. That is how men should be, instead of going round drenching the world with tears.

Wounds—yes, they are inflicted on almost everybody. People react differently. Some rise like a lion, shaking the manes, full of the spirit of revenge. Some forgive but do not forget. Yet others like Aparna just go on as if no wound has been inflicted.

Narendran has written a new poem in his blog titled 'The Wounded Deer':

I'm not going to sing of Mareecha,
The golden deer of Ramayana,
Sent by Ravana to lure Rama away from Sita.
After all, who is Mareecha, but a pimp?
I'm going to sing of a deer that resides in my heart.
The one whom I fed on dreams, desires and hopes
Like the sweet grass deer are fond of.
The one I kept in my heart, not letting anyone know.
That deer has been hurt, deeply wounded.

Aparna read it and told Narendran: 'Junior, you are growing up. I am happy that you have given up your efforts to write in metre.'

'What is wrong with writing in metre?' Narendran was irritated. 'Writers of movie songs compose to the tune set beforehand by others. And they are given national honours! Poets who write according to the metre are condemned! What justice is this?'

'I don't want to have another argument, please,' Aparna got up. 'I just said my opinion as you asked for it.'

'Don't go away Aparna,' Narendran stopped her by holding

her hand. 'Why don't you give me the freedom to justify myself?'

Aparna just gave a wry smile in return. 'Tell me, what else do you think? You know I value your comments.'

Aparna looked at the computer screen where the wounded deer stood, trying to bleed.

Who shot this arrow that has pierced your body?
Whose fingerprints are on it?
Among the many I recognize one.

'Shall I be frank?'Aparna asked.

'Please do. That is what I want.'

'I don't like the "I" in the poem. Why can't you writers think outside of yourself? Why can't you postpone your ego?'

'Well, I see myself as the deer.'

'Exactly. That is the problem. The deer has to come out crossing the bounds set by Narendran, the poet. Only then will the deer become everyone.'

'How can that be? Well, I don't think ...'

'Please do think. Meanwhile I will go make tea for us.'

Aparna went out of the room. She could not bring herself to like the several ways of Narendran. She had started feeling that she is being used as a whetstone to improve his poems, as a female body to wriggle under him in the nights. If the poet wonders whether he recognizes one of the fingerprints on the arrow darted at his deer, one can't blame the poet.

Chapter 3

Chats

Kashyap, I will be free from 6 to 8 in the evening today. Can you come on chat? Since Narendran's mother will be here, no Skype please.

Sure.

Kashyap reached the chat room by 6 and found Aparna waiting for him.

What a surprise! The woman bound by traditions is emancipated today!!

Hahaha. It was a bloodless revolution. A glorious one. Narendran is away on a reading session. You know, some poets' meet or something like that.

As a Pativrata or chaste wife, you should have accompanied him to the poets meet.

That applies to Pativratas only.

What happened Apu? Any problem?

I am fed up, Kashyap. We belong to the two poles.

But the poles met in a railway compartment and fell in love. What happened to that love?

There was no love. It was just a coincidence that I had to marry a fellow passenger from the past. You people teased me about it, but I had been telling you that there was no love. He might have felt drawn to me but it was only one-sided. I had never given him a second thought after we parted. Kashyap, all the serious demeanor he had put on in the train was only a show off, completely pretentious. When my mother showed me his photograph and I walked slowly into a life with him, I might have been dumb. Why didn't I see through him, the one who watched Turner and Hooch *quite seriously?*

What is wrong with watching Turner and Hooch*? I cannot agree with you, Apu. Even now if I get an evening off from my busy schedule I watch Pogo channel. Or I will read Walt Disney comics. It is not a sin, Apu, to like comedy. Don't you know that? Tom and Jerry can relieve your tension better than the works of any Nobel Prize winner.*

You take rest only after heavy work. Well-earned rest. Here it is the other way around. No work, only rest. The show-off man of the train can only talk meaninglessly.

Why do you always refer to him as show-off and pretentious? Anyway you did not marry him for his affected behaviour. You married him because your parents chose him for you. Forget the train journey. Instead of linking him to a meaningless past, why don't you place him in the present?

Something has to be there in the present to hold him in place.

Apu, my girl, you are behaving rather unkindly.

No Kashyap. I had never believed in Fate. But now I do.

Fate is a non-existent wall for a fool to lean on.

Wow! How sharp your words are, Kashyap!

Hahaha. Well, I must say that you are echoing the opinion of the world!

I wasn't joking, man. When I read your articles both online and in print media, I have always raised my eyebrows at the sharpness of your words and thoughts.

What lovely eyebrows!

Really, Kashyap. The way you nail the corrupt political leaders to the cross—I really admire your guts. I worship the path your pen treads. To tell you the truth, in my confrontations with the political leaders here, I imitate you sometimes. My model figure. I have always adored you.

What is the use of telling me all this now? You should have revealed your admiration for me before Narendran came to your life. He put a smiley of disappointment and tears here. *Oh, how unlucky I am!*

You naughty boy!

Aparna felt her mind relaxing slowly as the chat proceeded. The feeling of being back in the Delhi campus. Sitting opposite each other with steaming tea cups. Sharing views on everything under the sun. She forgot the other friends who had joined them. She tried to throw with force Neela Kalyani to the back of her mind. Neela was really the green-eyed monster, terribly possessive of Kashyap. She had literally choked him on the day she found Heidi Christian in his room. Heidi had come just to borrow some notes, but Kashyap had to face the fury of the woman scorned. *'No, I'm not angry at her,'* Kashyap said to Aparna later. *'One should understand psychology. It is all because of Neela's great love for me.'* Aparna had really wished then to have a lover who would be so understanding to see jealousy as the other side of the coin of love.

Now where is Neela with her great love? Aparna smiled to herself.

She chatted on, sharing everything she wanted to share—a tear drop at having to be the wife of a person so deeply narcissistic; a frown at his disgusting bed-habits; a melting away in her own helplessness; a pat on the shoulders of the channel-job that helps her to sustain; a protest against the husband's reaction that it is this job that fills her with self-pride; a fear of the depression that crawls slowly up her consciousness ...

Kashyap listened as Patience personified, revealing his sympathy and love through meaningful smileys. When Aparna-chirps seemed to be on the ebb, he said:

When I diagnose your words, the picture I get is different Apu. You have told me about your hard feelings towards Narendran, caused by himself. But, to me, the problem seems to spring from your great expectations. You expected too much from marriage. You are the Procrustes who waited for the ideal man to fit the bed.

Procrustes? Who is he? Or is it a she?

Haven't you heard of him? Procrustes, known in Greek mythology as the stretcher? He was a weird bandit. In his cave there was an iron bed. Whichever traveller he met will be brought there and enticed to lie down on the bed. Then he will set to work on their bodies with his smith's hammer. Suppose the man is short. Procrustes will stretch him by hammering or racking the body till it fits the length of the bed. If the body is longer than the bed, he will slice off the legs to make the body fit the size of the bed. In both cases the result would be death. He wanted a person who would be the actual size of the bed.

Did he ever get such a one?

Yes. Stories of people who never returned from the woods and of Procrustes, the stretcher, reached the palace. Prince Theseus, the young Attic hero, came looking for him to save his people. And Theseus turned out to be the correct size of the bed.

And then what happened?

What should happen? Theseus killed Procrustes by his own method.

Oh!

So my pretty one, stop being Procrustes who guards a bed, waiting for the ideal one to come. Marriage means lying with a partner who is not the size of the bed. You will never get the ideal one. Suppose you get one, the marriage will be short-lived. As Prince Theseus, the ideal one, brings only death with him. Procrustes had to die as soon as he got the ideal one.

Kashyap, you really amaze me. You are so changed!

I was always like this; but you never noticed me like that, that is all. May I add this too? Apu, if one judges using the yardsticks of society, Narendran is the ideal match for you. Handsome. Rich. Well-placed. Good family. No bad habits. A poet on his way to fame. All this counts with the people around. Planetary incompatibility they know, but mental incompatibility is a term that they have not come across. Anyway it is not a concrete concept; no one would understand it.

Yes, Kashyap, no one would understand. That is why my parents and brother never took my dissatisfaction seriously. It is impossible to live with a man who always turns around himself. Even when he plays with my body, his thoughts are self-centered. One day I will just go away leaving everything behind. How long can I go on deceiving myself like this?

Apu, darling, what has happened to you? Let me ask frankly. Were you in love with anyone else before marriage?

Aparna's fingers came to a standstill on the keyboard. Pradip + Bejoy Luxmi. Kashyap + Neela Kalyani. Aparna was always alone. She remembered with a surprise that no one has said 'I love you' to her even on Valentine's Day. In the campus almost all walked in pairs. Why was it that no one became her lover though she was good-looking? And, why didn't she feel its lapse ever?

Apu, are you there?

She did not reply.

Kashyap, with all his intellect and practical wisdom, must have known that Neela Kalyani, born with the silver spoon in her mouth, would never marry the son of a rickshaw-driver from the slums. Yet why didn't he turn his eyes to Aparna who stood solitary? Perhaps Aparna + Kashyap would have been a nice equation.

Hey Apu, Kashyap called. Some firecrackers exploded on the screen. *Are you sleeping? Wake up, my sleeping beauty!*

I am here alright.

But who ever loved Aparna? Narang with his pig-face? Narang had said that he had thought about their five-member gang; he did not say that he had thought about Aparna. His problem was who belonged to whom in the gang. Once he had trampled with Aparna's body, he had tried to show his affinity in many ways. For internals and projects he gave high marks to Aparna.

It was then that the class heard Sonjay Mithra's voice in anger, 'This is not fair, Professor. You are showing favouritism.'

Sonjay who ran to his room with shame from the condom-vending machine in the hostel! The silent cat that revealed sharp nails when countered.

Kashyap has typed many solaces and messages of self-courage. Not bothering to read them at all, Aparna asked him,

What is our Sonjay Mithra doing now? Do you have contact with him?

In the last phase of his training in Mussoorie. Most probably he will be posted in Calcutta. You know, he is the topper.

What about Narang? Our Professor?

I only know that he is outside India on sabbatical.

Oh!

You want to know only about these two? You are not bothered about anyone else?

Aparna sent a smiley as response.

So these two are the problems for you! Anyway you will never love Narang, I'm sure. No woman can. Was Sonjay ever in your dreams Apu? But I don't think that can happen. He is so much in love with himself that no one else can love him.

Kashyap, don't forget that I'm living with a minor edition of him. But no, dear, Sonjay had never even crossed my thoughts. My mind was full of only one person—that Tribal King. Hope you have not forgotten him.

A symbol of shock came to Aparna's chat room.

That dirty scoundrel? No, I don't believe it.

Why not? Did you see any unhappy woman in that colony? They were all full of love and energy. He was the Krishna who held them together. Yesterday I had a strange dream. The Tribal King came to my house. I asked him to come in. He did.

Oh. Was Narendran there? Or his mom? I mean, in your dream.

He wasn't there; but Amma was in the kitchen or prayer room, I don't remember. The Tribal King stood staring at me and stretched his hands to me.

I'm sure you ran away because of the foul smell.

No. I rushed into his arms. I realized that my life so far had been a wait for him. I wanted to be hugged by him; to be kissed...

Apu ...

Yes Kashyap; I wanted him desperately. Then we made love on Narendran's bed. I know I'm shocking you.

I'm not shocked; but I'm trying to get a clue to understand you.

There is no clue, don't bother. I woke up in a cold sweat and found Narendran snoring by my side.

Were you disappointed?

That would be the least to say.

I know you are joking, Aparna. But I wonder what you yearn for in your subconscious mind—the barbarian in the man?

Aparna sensed somebody behind her and turned suddenly to see Narendran standing very close to her. Immediately closing the screen, she got up.

'Amma told me that you were sitting in front of the computer from the time I left the house. Three hours! You refused to come with me to the poets' meet on the excuse that you had to do homework for tomorrow's shoot.'

She saw that Narendran was trying to control his anger. In a sweetened voice she said, 'True, I was doing my homework for tomorrow's programme. Typing away. I logged on only a few minutes ago. Neela Kalyani was on chat and she was telling me about one of her strange dreams.'

She took her mobile on the sly and switched it off while talking. Kashyap may call as the chat has ended abruptly.

'Sit here Narendran, and tell me how the poets' meet was,' She said trying to bring him around. 'Who all were there? Did you read only the poems we fixed yesterday? How were they taken? I'm sure they were well-received.'

Narendran visibly relaxed and accepted her invitation to sit. 'I read only two poems. Young poets will be called only after the so-called famous ones. I had to listen to the renditions of dyed hair poets in the traditional way. Disgusting they were! So old-fashioned; yet people clapped for them!'

'What about the younger poets?'

'I was the fifth one from among them to be called. The old poets had left the hall as soon as their poems were over. They cannot tolerate fresh ideas and new ways of expression. They think the world has to end with them. So we too followed suit. I came away as soon as my turn was over.'

'Then what is the difference between the older poets and you?'

'What do you mean?'

'I mean, you should have stayed on to listen to the others.'

'Aha! Only then could you have got more time to chat! Don't think that I am a fool.'

Aparna got up from her chair.

'I may have to chat for official purposes.'

'It was not an official chat that I saw on screen just now. I adjust very much to live with you, closing my eyes to many things. But don't take advantage of it.'

'Narendran, you are not the only who adjusts. Perhaps I'm the one who does it more than you.'

Before he could respond, Narendran's mobile started ringing. The ringtone was his poem in his own voice. He took the phone from the pouch on the belt and started speaking.

'Narendran here ... Oh? Thank you. Thank you .... Should you go that far? Ha ha ha ... Thanks again. May I know your name please? ... Swapna! Ah, what a good name! What do you do now? ... O my God, judging from your voice I thought you must be a student. Where do you teach? ... You should have introduced yourself there itself.'

Narendran looked at Aparna with revenge glowing in his eyes and walked out with the phone. As he walked out, he said sweetly to the voice at the other end: 'Oh, is that so? ... That is right, that is right.'

'No, that is wrong, that is wrong,' Aparna said in a mumble. Then she burst into wild laughter.

Chapter 4

Making of a Mother

When two people who used to sleep on the same bed withdraw to two beds in the same room, the world will not know, as the world cannot peep into bedrooms. When the world knocks at the front door, one need only open it with a smile and give a cup of tea. The world will go back with the feeling that God is in his heaven and all is right in this house.

Aparna was able to enjoy fully the bliss of sleep for the first time after marriage when the beds parted company. She threw her hand here, her leg there, stretched, turned on the belly and celebrated her freedom. In the darkness no hand would come in search of her breasts, squeeze them and suck them dry. No hand or leg would fall on her body heavily and break her sleep.

The channel had gifted her with a laptop and she used to sit with it in the balcony till she was sure that Narendran was asleep.

On that night she felt lonelier than ever. Kashyap had accompanied the President of India on a foreign tour as a member of the Press. So there was no one to chat with. Aparna went back to Kashyap's latest mail:

I am the youngest one in Rashtrapati's team. All people say that I am so lucky to be selected. It seems the President himself has asked them to take me. He might have read my articles. You know I never go in search of laurels or recognition. I just do my duty, but take care that I do it well. This has come my way without any effort from my side, though some among the Fourth Estate think otherwise. I just pity them. My father used to tell all of us right from our childhood to do our duties well—be it that of a cart-driver or of a student. He has asked us not to worry about the rewards; they might or might not come; but that could not be an excuse for not doing one's duty. Apu, my father is not educated; he has not read Bhagavad Gita. He does not even know that such a text exists.

Aparna wondered whether Kashyap had run into Neela Kalyani somewhere in the United States. Neela who is now after him in the Mills and Boon way.

Aparna, I googled Kashyap's name. Neela Kalyani had written in a recent mail. *To say surprised conveys the least; I had never realized that he was such a potential person! I felt like coming over to India to give him a hug. May be I should have stayed there and found a journalistic profession so that I could also be as well-known. I am fed up staying confined to the apartment. Utham has found a solution to lead me out of my complaints and boredom: he says I must think of becoming a mother. That will make his life easy. I will have no time even to make complaints. Cleaning the baby's shit, changing the diapers, doing research on baby-talk, I would be the ideal wife that Utham wants me to be. I told him curtly, no, not in the near future. By the way, did you know, our Bejoy Luxmi is carrying ....*

Reading the letter again, Aparna felt that she must congratulate Bejoy Luxmi. She started searching among the online cards and found one. A basket. Click the mouse over it and a lot of toys spring out. And one hears the cry and laughter of the mother and child. Aparna wrote her message, *The hand that rocks the cradle rules the world. Be a benign ruler, my dear friend!* She sent the card and the response came almost immediately from Bejoy Luxmi.

Apu, how did you know? I'm surprised! Thank you dear, thanks ever so much. So we, the unmarried couple are going to be parents. My mom compels us to get married; Pradip's parents are equally stubborn that the holy knot has to be tied. They are scared that the children born otherwise would be termed bastards. In the US, it does not matter; but in India it matters a lot, especially to conservative families. What they don't understand is that the US is not like India. Here people live together and when the baby comes, they just go and register in the government office that the child is theirs. No problem after that. But these old people can't understand. Anyway Pradip and I do not hate marriage as such; we have nothing against it. Delhi had made us rebel against the existing system, that is all. What difference is marriage going to make to our lives? We may or may not get married.

Tell me when can I send a similar card to you?

Aparna sat thoughtfully. In the early stages of Aparna's marriage, Narendran's mother used to talk about the need of a baby in the house; but of late she had stopped it. Maybe the Mom's boy must have told her about the distance between the two beds. Yes, that must be the reason why she spends more time in the Pooja room and comes out with tear-soaked red eyes.

Aparna felt contempt towards herself.

After an outdoor programme, the channel team landed at the Indian Coffee House to have tea and *masala dosa.*

'Aparna, you are not in a good mood today. Am I correct?'

'What makes you think so, Dileep?'

'Well your questions seemed to lack the usual spark and punch. You seemed to be in a mood to compromise. As the Malayalam writer VKN asked, "Where is the fire in you?"'

'Do you need a VKN to ask that question? It was a common query heard in the Delhi campus.'

'I was just curious if you had any problem; wondering if I can help in any way.'

'Dileep, Aparna cannot have any problem in life,' Samad, the camera-man laughed aloud. 'Her poet-engineer-husband is such a good man that if at all there is any problem, it would be created by Aparna alone.'

'You get lost,' Aparna faked anger at Samad. As she swallowed her *masala dosa* in a hurry, she asked herself whether the anger was real or faked. Dileep felt bad that he had created the situation.

It stirred a world of thoughts in Aparna. *What is it that extinguishes the fire in me? The beds that have moved apart? The absence of Kashyap?*

An award in the name of a person no one has heard of, came in search of Narendran. The place where the award function was going to be held was so far away that half of the award money would have to be spent to reach there. Aparna opined that if the award-giving ceremony takes place at long distances, the award committee should mete out TA/DA as well. Narendran frowned at her in anger.

'I don't give much importance to the cash given,' he said. 'You know me better than that. An award in recognition of your work is an honour conferred upon you! I will go there even if it is in the name of someone not well-known.'

Later he stood in the middle of the two beds and spoke to the air: 'They have asked me to come with family. Why can't you come with me? Otherwise, misunderstandings would arise. I don't want the press talking low of me as I am on my way to fame and reputation.'

Aparna suppressed her laughter. It was one of the lesser-noticed awards. The news of the award has appeared in a remote corner in the newspapers where no reader would naturally reach.

Then the winner of the award telephoned the press. *'Why haven't you published my photograph? That is the usual practice for such awards!'*

He is curtly told: *'We don't usually publish the photograph of the award winner if the cash prize is so little. But we will put it, if you will give the charges of an advertisement.'*

The award winner compromises. *'That is Ok. But can you put it in such a manner that it does not appear as an advertisement?'*

The press consents. *'OK. We will treat this as a special case; but the charge would be more.'*

The cash is delivered immediately. The next day's newspapers carry the photograph with the news:

Narendran, winner of...award for the best young poet of the year.

And the poet thinks he is on the way to 'fame and reputation.' What fame! And, what reputation!

Seeing Aparna who alighted from the car with Narendran, some people whispered, 'Isn't this the girl we see on the news channel?'

'Yes, the one always with the mike.'

'The one who shoots questions at all our leaders?'

'Yes, Aparna Narendran! I remember how she cornered our Chief Minister the other day.'

'Oh, so the award-winner is her husband!'

Aparna knew that Narendran would die of an ego-attack if he heard the words. He does not want to be known as 'her husband'; he wants Aparna to be known as Narendran's wife. As if there is such a gulf between the two expressions!

The speakers were seated on the stage in two rows. Aparna saw that they were just some minor figures in politics and some local writers. Narendran was given a seat at the right end in the front row. Why so many speakers just to present a poet with an award? Aparna felt that some rule should be enforced to limit the number of speakers on all stages. From her front-row seat among the audience she watched Narendran being given the award by a local politician who claimed to be the branch secretary of some party. Aparna took photographs on her tablet and saw that Narendran was looking his brightest as he smiled and held the memento in his hands.

She was really irritated at the speakers who were literally in love with the mike. As they cracked local jokes, the audience roared with laughter, but the essence of the jokes refused to come to Aparna. She saw that Narendran was also making the pretence of smiling, as he also could not understand where the joke lay. She texted Narendran: *It is getting quite late. Please tell the organizers that we have a long distance to travel to get back home. Ask them to allow you to express thanks and liberate you.*

Narendran looked at Aparna with a frown and switched off his mobile. He placed it back in the pouch on his belt and pretended to pay attention to the speakers.

Finally, after 9 o'clock the organizers allowed the poet to speak a few words. The formal Vote of Thanks was the only item left in the programme chart. Each speaker had left the stage and the venue after his speech; so the stage was almost empty. In the audience there were more empty chairs than human beings. Some man started piling the empty chairs one on top of the other; maybe he was the one who provided them.

Narendran came to the mike. After the formal address—he addressed all the speakers who had left the stage, making Aparna look away with disgust—he began:

> “
>
> I wanted to read one or two poems of mine here, but, as we have already exceeded the time and as we have a long way to go to get back home, I am not doing it. I thank sincerely the jury who selected me for this award and the organizers who have arranged this wonderful function. (*Wonderful!* Aparna smirked!) The poet in me has been created and perfected by my family, my home, my parents and my teachers. I remember each of them now with gratitude.

This is the second award I have received so far. After the first award a sincere and harsh critic has come to my life. My poems have come out better, rubbed on the whetstone of that friend. So I dedicate this award to my best friend, my wife, Aparna Narendran. ”

The audience clapped. Some of them turned and stretched their necks to look at her. Aparna sat jolted at this unexpected turn of events. When she came back to herself after a minute, Narendran was reciting his latest poem, which she had not yet seen.

The wick was flittering on the earthen lamp,
When you came to me with fresh fire.
Colourful my life turned all of a sudden.
You showed me the sights I had never seen,
You made me listen to music unheard so far.

Dear, you told me not to look for poems
In rainbows, flowers and butterflies;
You showed me the hue when hope
Is reflected on the teardrops of the trodden.

I dedicate to you my whole world,
All my poems, my tears and smiles,
Dear, my life and even my death
I lay at your feet, my goddess of poetry!

As he walked back to his chair on the dais Narendran lifted his small finger to the corner of his eyes. Aparna noticed that he was sitting with a serious countenance, without even looking at her. And, surprising herself, she found a maternal tenderness spreading over her body and mind.

They did not talk to each other while travelling in the car. Even while having *thattudosa* and tea from the wayside shop, they did not break the silence.

Aparna lay back on her seat watching Narendran drive. She wished he would turn to look at her at least once. But he seemed to concentrate on driving. Aparna kept on looking at his side view for quite a long time. Is it possible to return this love, ever? He does not know that she had walked into his life with a polluted body. Perhaps if he knew it, his poetry would have changed—maybe into something better. As she watched him without his knowing, a soft tenderness descended on her and enveloped her.

Needless to say, the beds rejoined in their room that night.

Kashyap, yesterday Narendran bought a pregnancy tester. A drop of urine on it showed a positive result. I am going to be a mother! I know it is not a piece of news value that a married woman of my age is going to be a mother. It is the price we have to pay for the folly of a moment. But you should have seen the reaction of Narendran. He seemed to ascend the Himalaya of ecstasy. To tell you the truth, I could not share his excitement.

Shall I tell you a story, Kashyap, which you have never known? Once, I had done this pregnancy test in the privacy of my hostel room in Delhi. My rising heartbeats took some time to come down even after seeing the negative result. Yet when the menstrual periods delayed to come I burned away. I started believing that there is a live foetus in my womb. I started doing rigorous exercises to destroy it— running up and down the stairs, rigorous work-outs in the gym. Yet the crimson flower refused to bloom. I repeated the test and again the result was negative. I really felt that the man's semen had sowed the seeds of cancer in my womb, the growth of it blocking the menstrual blood. But one day, as I was in an auto rickshaw coming to Pradip's room to watch his project-movie, blood drops rolled down my thighs.

It was a period of great mental turmoil for me. None of you even sensed it.

And now the guest has really come to my uterus.

Kashyap's response was a single question:

Was it Sonjay who was behind the pregnancy tests in Delhi?

No. Aparna replied. *The question 'Who' is quite irrelevant. What is relevant is another question. Why did I yield, without even a mild protest, to a man with an ugly face? When he touched me, I remember I never felt any romantic wave on my body. My body just silently gave in. And he was a person I never cared for, I never even thought of.*

Kashyap sent a grin smiley and wrote,

Let me take 'a man with an ugly face' as clue and quickly make a mental tour through our campus. Hey, who has got a more ugly face than I? But, to the best of my belief we never went through such an experience. Apu, ha haha, it is only a joke, ok?

Kashyap, you have the freedom to crack any joke to me or at me. But don't ever say that you are ugly. You are one of the most attractive men I have ever seen. We should have met more often; we should have known each other better.

Apu, it is foolish to ruminate on what could have been. I had always liked you; in fact I was your fan. I had respected you also. You were always very cool, never flippant as I used to be. You say none of us knew the times of your mental turmoil. You are wrong. At that time we sensed something was wrong, that you were under high pressure. We had talked about it in your absence. All of us thought it must be due to some problem at home. You had never given us any reason to think otherwise. But, who was the trickster who made you do the pregnancy tests? Aparna chose not to reply.

She felt a sense of irritation mounting in her at the extreme care she was receiving at home. Narendran's mother cooked only the dishes that Aparna liked. Sometimes she would turn up new dishes as surprises for her pregnant daughter-in-law. Since they were all delicious and since Aparna never had any sickness, she used to enjoy them to the full. Any daughter-in-law's dream of a mother-in-law, alright. But Aparna felt disgusted that she was always after her, asking, 'Can you feel the kicks of the baby now? Does the baby ask you to tell the grandma to make caramel pudding?' She felt like saying 'Don't you have anything else to do?' In fact she asked that to Narendran when he was rubbing his nose on her navel, talking to the baby. He was sure that it was going to be a girl, while his mother was too sure that it would be a boy. 'Does it matter?' Aparna felt like asking. 'Does anything matter?'

What mattered to her most was her privacy. But with an overcaring husband and mother-in-law she was losing it fast. Narendran's mother used to try her patience with queries and observations like,

'Is it ok for pregnant ladies to use the mobile for a long time like this? Won't it affect the baby ...?', 'Are you sure you can sit long like this in front of the computer? Won't the radiation reach the child?', 'I think you should give up travelling by scooter ... Please don't climb the stairs often; it might exert pressure on the baby.'

Aparna never reacted till her mother-in-law reached the limits, and that was when she said that Aparna should resign the job in the News Channel. Narendran too supported his mother. He pointed out the example of Supriya, Aparna's colleague, who had to run when the protestors in front of the secretariat turned riotous. She fell down and people just tread upon her. When the cameraman lifted her from the ground, she was all blood. That had been a favourite topic of discussion in the channels; they went on showing Supriya's bleeding body being supported by the cameraman.

'Suppose something like that happens!' Narendran said in apprehension. 'I think it is better to follow Amma's advice. Anyway you have proved your level grade in the channel. So after delivery it won't be difficult for you to get another good job.'

Aparna grumbled to herself, 'Yes, now delivering the child ... next, breastfeeding the child ... No, I will not be tied to the house. I won't resign.'

As a last resort Aparna complained to her parents. But both of them advised her to follow what the husband and his people say.

'Blast you,' Aparna said in her mind. 'Blast all of you!'

Bejoy Luxmi told Aparna that she has named their child Peeyush. She said that in two months' time she would be coming to Delhi with Peeyush Lahiri and Pradip Lahiri. Since Kashyap is in Delhi, she suggested that Aparna also come to Delhi so that they can have a reunion.

'You are not going to any place, let alone Delhi,' Narendran said. 'Long-distance travel may be harmful to the baby.'

'Let the doctors say that Narendran. You are not a doctor. At this stage of pregnancy I don't think travelling is dangerous.'

'Let the doctors say that,' said Narendran with a wry smile.

'Why are you so adamant? I am not going to meet any lover from the past. I never had any. Why don't you also come with me?' Aparna invited him.

'Oh, thanks,' Narendran made no attempt to hide his scorn. 'I am not at all interested in seeing your old friends.'

Aparna placed her right hand on her swelling belly. *'So you are the snag. Even before you come out, you take away my little freedoms one by one. Will you be chaining my hands and feet once you come out?'*

The baby hit her hard with a little paw to show its protest.

Aparna reintroduced the topic later in the peace of the night in the bedroom. But Narendran became angrier than ever.

'You will never go with my consent. I clearly remember what you had told me in the train—that you know very well where you want to go and how to get there. But if anything happens to my baby while you travel or celebrate, you will be solely responsible. And you don't have to come back after that.'

Aparna felt that she was created with the sole purpose of carrying Narendran's child inside her to be properly brought out. A kangaroo that is denied the privilege of hopping about, just because there is a child in the pouch! She felt that everything she had done was wrong. She should not have left Delhi in the first place. Who was she scared of? Was she scared that the pig-faced Narang would come after again? If she hated him so much, why should she carry his memories with her even now? If only she had accepted the job offer of *The Economic Times* and continued in Delhi, she might have met a buddy somewhere on the wayside, someone who could share her world of ideas too. Maybe Kashyap would have come to her, the Kashyap, abandoned by Neela Kalyani.

'Aparna,' Narendran touched her shoulders with love and tenderness. 'Why do you behave like this, dear? What do you lack in this house? We are going to be parents. Think of the happiness the child will bring to this house. And remember, even a small negative thought will influence the baby at this stage.'

'Take your baby and go to hell,' Aparna said to Narendran without words.

Chapter 5

The Holy Family

Aparna is within a dream now.

Inside the dream she travels in a train. Like reality turned upside down, Narendran sits in the compartment engrossed in a book, while Aparna sits with a laptop, playing Angry Birds.

Chinnu asks Aparna, *'Aunty, why do you have a bulging tummy?'* Aparna pretends not to hear it.

Chinnu asks again, *'Do you have a little baby in your tummy? Look at this Minnu. She was in my mother's tummy, and her tummy had also bulged out like this. But when Minnu came out, the bulge went off, like gas from a balloon.'*

The Jeans-mom calls her back with the words, *'Hey Chinnu, don't disturb Aunty. She has to give us her lower berth later.'*

Narendran, sitting near Aparna, whispers in her ears, *'Do you really have a baby inside?'*

'*Yes,*' Aparna whispers back.

'Who is the father?' Narendran asks curiously. *'Narang or Kashyap?'*

Aparna replies, *'No, the Tribal King.'*

'Who is the Tribal King?' Narendran asks.

'Every Woman's Man,' says Aparna. *'He who sees no difference in any woman. The First Man and the Last Man.'*

'Where is he to be found?' Narendran wants to know.

'In the next compartment,' says Aparna.

Aparna and Narendran steal to the next compartment, opening the door cautiously, not disturbing the sleeping Jeans-mom and her children.

There the Tribal King reigns, fondled by innumerable women. Unkempt dirty hair and body smeared with dust, but surrounded by women beautiful and not. Aparna notices that some of the women were her classmates. She calls out to them. *'Hi Cynthia! Hi Aditya! Neela! Hello Parul! Gayu, don't you know me? Hello Teji, I am Apu!'* But no one even looks at her.

The Tribal King speaks: *Rape always had a patriarchal centre and butterfly effect. But I have never raped a woman. I can enjoy a woman only if she comes with an open heart. I have never hurt a woman. That is why all these women love me like this.*

Shouting *'You Cheat!'* Aparna raises the Tribal King from his seat and throws him out of the window. He does not fall down, but hovers in the air. Suddenly a rain breaks out and the water washes off the mud and dust from his body, making him a really handsome man. Narang walks into the compartment with a text in hand and begins reading: *'Beware, the Prince of Darkness comes as a gentleman.'*

The clean and handsome Tribal King sits near Aparna and writes down the lecture notes. *'The Prince of ....'* He asks Aparna—*'Does darkness has one s or two?'*

'Three,' Aparna replies.

And the Tribal King writes, *'The Prince of Darknesss.'*

Aparna feels drawn to his magnetic field and leans to him. Now her fingers are running through his abundant chest hair. Bejoy Luxmi appears at the door with a baby strapped to her body. The baby's face is like the Tribal King's. *'Sorry, Professor Narang,'* she says. *'The flight from the US was late, so kindly excuse me.' 'Alright come in,'* says Narang. *'Don't ever repeat it.'* Bejoy Luxmi comes and sits near Aparna. Aparna extends her hand to stroke the child's hair, but withdraws it, seeing the Tribal King's grin on the child's face. She turns away from the child.

In her dream Aparna moved dangerously to the side of the bed. She would have fallen, but a child's apprehensive cry in the dream –'Amma, don't!' stopped her in time. When she opened her eyes she saw that she was about to fall down, caught herself and withdrew her body just in time.

She stroked her bulging tummy softly and asked, *'Did you wake me up, my darling?'*

Narendran woke up at that moment, turned to her, and asked 'Did you say anything just now?'

'No,' said she, while muttering to herself, *'Does not this man sleep at all?'*

Narendran gently reminded her, 'Aparna, hasn't the doctor told you not to lie on your back? Please turn to the left; that posture is the good one for the child.'

'Shut up,' Aparna glared in her mind. *'The child! The child! Always the child! Why don't you think of me at least once in a while? Tell me what is good for me also, the slave that I am!'*

Suddenly Narendran's voice became alert: 'Aparna, is there any problem? You are sweating. Are you OK?'

Aparna shouted loudly, 'Don't switch on the light please.'

Narendran's fingers withdrew automatically from the switch.

Aparna got up from the bed, wondering what she was dreaming of. The image of the child that resembled the Tribal King came to her mind veiled as a shadow. How can the baby of Pradip Lahiri and Bejoy Luxmi resemble the Tribal King?

People say that all children look alike when they are newborn babes. Maybe, when her child is born, will s/he also bear the semblance of the Tribal King? Will all the children in the world resemble him?

'Aparna, are you alright? Is there any problem? Why don't you say something?'

She was terribly irritated at Narendran's probing questions.

'I just want to go to the toilet. Don't I have the freedom to do even that?'

She sipped from the water bottle on the table after her return from the toilet and lay on the bed, fully aware of the alert eyes of Narendran on her. She lay on her left side to avoid more instructions and reminders.

Her dream lay scattered all over her mind. As sleep eluded her, she tried to pick up the snippets of the dream. The Tribal King, cleansed by the rain, bore resemblance to Abram Uncle. The Abram Uncle who never touched her or patted her or stroked her chin—not even once. But unless she is able to collect all the scattered pieces, how can she put the jigsaw puzzle together?

When she heard Narendran softly snoring, Aparna got up from the bed again. She took her laptop and walked to the balcony.

Yes, Narang was there in the dream. Umakant Narang was teaching in the classroom. The Tribal King sat near Aparna, busy taking down notes. Aparna tried to recall the person who used to sit near her in the class. Sometimes it was Neela Kalyani. When she was absent—she had more days of absence than of presence—someone else used to move to her place. Who was that? However much she tried, Aparna could not bring that face back to mind. It was never Kashyap or Pradip, not even Bejoy Luxmi. Some anonymous person.

Bejoy Luxmi had sent a photograph to Aparna's mail, a photo that she had titled 'The Newborn Father'. While waiting for the picture to download, Aparna thought of Luxmi's mail describing the labour room experiences—how Pradip was with her during the delivery, holding her hand and stroking her forehead, repeating the doctor's instructions, watching the baby's journey outside of the womb. She had not sent any picture with that mail.

Aparna enlarged the photo.

Bejoy Luxmi lying on the white-sheeted hospital bed with the fatigue of having delivered a child writ large on her face. The little baby lying on her chest with face upwards, in deep sleep. Aparna noticed Bejoy Luxmi's eyes were also half-closed; but they looked more charming that way. Then there was, of course, Pradip Lahiri, the proud father, wearing a surgical mask. His eyes were bright with happiness. He had placed one hand on the child and another on the forehead of his wife, and was looking at the camera with extreme joy and pride.

'Here is our unholy family,' Bejoy Luxmi had written under it.

Aparna kept on looking at the unholy family. The tired Bejoy Luxmi was looking at the camera with her head slightly tilted to one side. She was trying to smile. Eyes were dazed with sleep and looked dreamy. Aparna wondered whether the hospitals here will place the newborn baby on the chest of the mother and allow photographs to be taken with the father by the side.

'Whose photo is this?'Narendran asked softly. As if by reflex action, the slightly startled Aparna minimized the window.

'It is my friend Bejoy Luxmi. She is in Australia now.'

'Oh? May I see that photo once again please?'

She enlarged the window showing her irritation very clearly on her face.

'One minute,' he said and invited himself to the laptop. 'No,' Aparna tried to prevent him. 'What are you going to do? Please don't delete it.'

'Delete?' Narendran smiled. 'Will anyone feel like deleting such a beautiful picture? I have just forwarded it to my mail.'

'Why?'Aparna looked at him with suspicion.

'Just because I like it,' said Narendran with a smile and walked away. In a minute he returned with his laptop and sat opposite Aparna.

'You go ahead with what you were doing,' he told Aparna. 'I have some work to do.'

'Look Narendran, please don't send anything to her mail,' Aparna was really disturbed. But Narendran laughed very loudly.

'Aparna, my sweet idiot, do you think I am such a fellow? Have I ever struck you like that?' With the words he turned to the computer.

Aparna sat for a while with doubts running through her mind. But since Narendran sat immersed in work and never even darted a glance at her, she returned to the other mails in the inbox.

The green light in the chat told her that Kashyap was online. It was past midnight; not his working hours. When he works, his chat is always switched off. She casually threw a glance at Narendran, found him immersed in some work, and then sent a 'Hi' to Kashyap. Pat came the reply.

Apu! What a surprise! Why are you online at this late hour? Time you should be sleeping peacefully. Pregnant women should not stay awake at this time.

Is that so? Why are you here now? The rule you mentioned applies to the friends of pregnant women too.

Hahaha! That is a nice one. To tell you the truth, I'm in an interesting chat now. A lady journalist whom I met in the United States has become an ardent admirer of mine. A very intellectual young lady. She has an answer for every question; a solution for any problem. To be frank, at some of her questions I have to resort to silence as I have no answer.

As Aparna had nothing to say, she sent a smiley as reply. Had there been no such emoticons, it would have been really difficult in certain contexts.

Beauty and wisdom is a rare combo—especially in women. Wendy has both of them more than enough. Why don't you visit my Facebook page? You can see her profile there. Her charming photo also.

Are you in love with her?

Well ... not at the moment. But if things go like this, I may fall headlong in love. Tonight we are chatting about Ashtangamarga of Sri Budhdha; in fact I am teaching her.

OK, proceed, honourable Guru. Goodnight.

Goodnight Apu. Go, have a good sleep. You have to look after yourself so well now, don't you know? Pamper yourself a bit even.

Aparna signed off, wondering why she was slightly upset about the whole thing. How can Mrs Aparna Narendran ever hope for Kashyap to remain a bachelor? Aparna sighed and took in a long breath. May Kashyap be not disappointed in this love affair at least!

She had started feeling sleepy. With a yawn she closed the laptop and got up.

'One minute,' Narendran called her. 'Just have a look at this,' He turned his laptop towards her.

He had edited Bejoy Luxmi's unholy family in Photoshop and made it his own.

The face of the person lying on the bed was Aparna's. It was a face taken from their marriage album—one with a bright smile. He had cut off the tired face of Bejoy Luxmi and pasted Aparna's face there. The babe on her chest had no face; it was edited off. Pradip Lahiri's face was replaced with Narendran's. Narendran was standing without any surgical mask, placing one of his hands on the child and another on Aparna's forehead. His face beamed, radiating happiness.

A play of transposed heads! Aparna stood looking hard at it. 'But why did you remove the child's face?'

'It is their child. Ours is only going to be born. We will know how he or she looks only after seeing the baby. Once the baby arrives, this picture will go to the Photoshop again.'

As she looked at the transformed photograph, Aparna felt the weapons slipping off her hands. The roused motherly instincts made her a helpless Durga with empty hands. But it was only for a moment. Aparna sprang back to herself in the next. She will not allow anyone to keep her under lock and key just because she is going to be a mother. The reunion in Delhi has to take place.

She was confused at her own bickering selves. As she stood, her eyes glued to the child without a face on her chest, Narendran put his hands round her shoulders and gently led her to the bedroom.

'Turn on the left side and go to sleep,' Narendran told her. 'Let our baby have a calm and sound sleep.'

The Story Ends

Kamala-4

Kamala finished reading the novel half an hour before the train reached the station. She had to pause at four places to finish her puri breakfast and attend three phone calls.

The first call was Amma's. *'Dad was talking about you in the night before going to sleep, and, as usual, had suffocation and discomfort in the chest. He did not allow us to take him to the hospital. He asks why should he prolong his life like this?... Dear, we haven't believed the rumours people spread about you—that you are living in an open relationship. But please be kind to your loving parents ...'*

When mother started crying, Kamala cut the conversation, pretending that the train had reached the station.

The second call was from Sidan. After the usual questions like 'Did you sleep well? How was the breakfast?' Sidan became serious: 'Kamu, I have to tell you something which I cannot share here at our place. I have given much thought to it, and, please don't tease me. I am really thinking of marrying you. I know it is a violation of our ideology, but I have to admit that this is how

I feel now, ideology or not .... Now, don't say anything; just let me finish. I had been sort of haunted by this idea of marriage for quite some time; maybe that is the reason why I missed you a lot this time. The sadness and longing I had while you were gone—is that what is called love? I don't know as I haven't loved anyone. Long before, I had resented your close interactions with Vinu—I suppressed it, as it would go against the ideal on which we have built up our relations. But I can't bear it any more. Ok, now, have your say.'

'Do you realize what you are saying, Sidan? We had planned everything before we started living together—we had planned even our old age. How can you deceive the Fourcentric gang?'

'You are right, but I can't help it. I have to be true to myself. You have to be mine. I want to be happy with you and you alone. Anyway think about it.'

The third and fourth calls were from fellow researchers. Those calls came when Aparna and Narendran were sitting in the balcony—Aparna with her chat and Narendran with his Photoshop. Kamala finished those two calls in a hurry to turn to the last page of the novel.

To fall into an incompatible marriage is like falling into the narrow pit between the train and the platform and feeling suffocated. That was what Aparna was going through. If Kamala were to accept Sidan's proposal, she would also land in the same pit. She thought of the Fourcentric flat with four bedrooms. Everyone gets his / her privacy in abundance. No one can say who was with whom in the previous night as no slipper would be left outside. And one is not supposed to knock at any door after 12 in the night. The etiquette demands that no questions are asked.

The Sidan whom she has known till now may not be the Sidan after marriage. Possessiveness is the greatest vice in any relationship. The Sidan who talked loud against the green-eyed monster says: *'I had resented your close interactions with Vinu.'*

Which prison is waiting for me, Kamala asked herself. Whether she yields to him or not, the inevitable is bound to happen. The end of the Fourcentrics.

She looked at the title page of the novel.

Invisible Walls

It should have been titled *The Prison-Houses of Aparna!*

Kamala took the pen from her bag and wrote under the title:

(Closing in)

She withdrew her mind from disturbing thoughts.

Now there is only one truth; not Bakthian multiples, but one. The Truth is this compartment in the train. It is Govind who is sleeping with his face fallen on his chest. The truth is the matured couple who sit immersed in silence.

The train had stopped moving and Govind woke up with a jerk. Kamala jumped to the platform with her backpack.

Govind who got down after her asked, 'Where do you want to go? Need my help?'

Kamala wondered whether she should say like Aparna. *'No, thanks. I know very well where I want to go and how to get there.'* But she chose not to. Instead she said, 'No, thanks. I can get there by myself.'

'This is my card,' Govind handed her his visiting card. 'You can call me anytime if you want my help or company.'

'Sure,' said Kamala.

When she found out that Govind was stalling to walk with her, Kamala pretended to receive a phone call and stood there rooted, talking. Govind waited for a minute and then moved on at a slow pace, turning back occasionally to look. She continued her pretence of talking till he melted in the crowd. And then she started walking forward, throwing his card into the space between the train and the platform.

From the compartment right in front of her, a man was helping a pregnant woman to alight. Kamala noticed that the lady's feet were swollen.

As soon as she stepped onto the platform the pregnant woman started talking on her mobile 'Yea, we reached right now. So you all are at Hotel Qutab, right? Have they sent the car for picking us up? ... Oh, it is waiting outside? Ok, we will reach now.'

The man with her was protecting her from the jostling crowd with his one arm around her while with the other he was pulling the trolley.

'Don't hurry, please,' he told the woman. 'Let us wait till the crowd is gone. Any way the hotel people will wait.'

'No, Narendran,' said the woman. 'My friends are all waiting for us.'

'So what? Let them wait. I have put up with all your arrogance so far. Don't put on me the last straw that would break my tolerance. Suppose you get some infection from the crowd, it will affect my unborn child. We will wait here for a while and then move on slowly.'

But the pregnant woman kept on walking and he had to helplessly tag along with her. Kamala saw that the lady was in a hilarious mood, too ecstatic to be beyond the hurt that he could inflict on her.

Kamala looked at them with sympathy and walked on briskly.